PLACES FAR FROM ELLESMERE

N

PLACES FAR FROM ELLESMERE

a geografictione

EXPLORATIONS ON SITE

Aritha van Herk

Red Deer College Press

Second Printing 1990

The Publishers

Red Deer College Press

56 Avenue & 32 Street, Box 5005

Red Deer, Alberta, Canada, T4N 5H5

Credits

Cover Illustration: Scott Barham

Design & Typesetting: Boldface Technologies Inc.

Printed & Bound in Canada by Gagné Printing

Acknowledgements

"Calgary, this growing graveyard" first appeared in *NeWest Review* (December, 1987). It subsequently appeared in *a/long prairie lines, An Anthology of Long Prairie Poems*, edited by Daniel S. Lenoski. Winnipeg: Turnstone, 1989.

The publishers gratefully acknowledge the financial contribution of the Alberta Foundation for the Literary Arts, Alberta Culture and Multiculturalism, the Canada Council, Red Deer College and Radio 7 CKRD.

Canadian Cataloguing in Publication Data

van Herk, Aritha, 1954-

Places Far From Ellesmere

ISBN 0-88995-060-1

I. Title.

PS593.A545P62 1990 C813'.54 C90-091421-1

PR9199.3.V36P62 1990

FOR ELLESMERE,

THAT IT WILL STAY, ETERNALLY, MYSTERIOUSLY,

ITS OWN GEOGRAFICTIONE

Thanks to:

The Glenbow Archives

Alberta Provincial Museum Library

Bezal and Terry Jesudason of Resolute Bay

Rudy Wiebe for the map

Dennis Johnson for his patience and for insisting on Edberg

Nicole Markotic for her inky fingers

Robert Sharp for Ellesmere

CONTENTS

Was that what travel meant? An exploration of the deserts of memory, rather than those around me?

– Claude Levi Strauss, *Tristes Tropiques*

A discursive formation is not, therefore, an ideal, continuous, smooth text that runs beneath the multiplicity of contradictions, and resolves them in the calm unity of coherent thought; nor is it the surface in which, in a thousand different aspects, a contradiction is reflected that is always in retreat, but everywhere dominant. It is rather a space of multiple dissensions; a set of different oppositions whose levels and roles must be described.

– Michel Foucault, *The Archaeology of Knowledge*

There are no more deserts. There are no more islands. Yet there is a need for them. In order to understand the world, one has to turn away from it on occasion; in order to serve [wo]men better, one has to hold them at a distance for a time. But where can one find the solitude necessary to vigour, the deep breath in which the mind collects itself and courage gauges its strength. There remain big cities. Simply, certain conditions are required.

– Albert Camus, "The Minotaur or The Stop in Oran"

[In the explorations of memory and place lie unsolved murders; in the multiple dissensions of distance and time, certain conditions prevail. The world admits deserts and islands but no women.]

N

EXPLORATION SITE : EDBERG

EDBERG, coppice of desire and return

Home: what you visit and abandon: too much forgotten/too much remembered. An asylum for your origins, your launchings and departures, the derivations of your dream geographies. Where you invented destinations. Always and unrelentingly (home) even after it is too late to be or to revert to (home), even after it pre/occupies the past tense.

A welt in the parkland on the raise between Dried Meat Lake and Meeting Creek, just off the Donalda/Duhamel trail: snagged between clumps of poplar and willow, the steady infusion of a prairie vapour from the everywhere tenacious low-growing rose bushes.

Edberg poised on a short, blunt-nosed hill up from the square grid of section lines, of homesteaded homesteaders already swinging through their fourth or fifth or sixth (who's counting?) generations, settlement in the plowed-to-dust bones and maybe-grandfathers who would utter if they remembered a different vowel, hailing themselves from restless settlers trickled out over the northwest like sand from a fist.

Under the long-painted houri eye of the prairie sky, past the whispered vigilance of cat-tail sloughs, the fence post boundaries marking their rusty decades, and the old model-A settling into a pyre of scrap in a corner of the bush (home). There might have been a trail passed here, that cart trail through this region partly wooded and with scattered trees and coppice (J.B. Tyrrell, 1887) once, a trail that angled across the sections and quarter-sections without the ninety-degree angles of the survey crews (their muscled arms, their chains, their principles of scrutiny), a trail that led between communities, between schools, between stopping places and boarding houses (with their lice and good company), between general stores, between horse-barns. You won't mention beer parlours. You've never crossed the doorsill of the Edberg beer parlour, still, silently forbidden to you even after several ages of consent.

Or the one in Meeting Creek, either, for that matter (gone now), or New Norway, or Ferintosh, or Bashaw, or Rosalind. First place you touched draught was Edmonton, well it might have been stampede Stettler or Ponoka but it wasn't Edberg.

But the cars and half-tons angled in front of the Edberg Hotel still display a silent declaration of indolence and afternoon: what makes men enter such ripe darkness in the middle of bright summer haying? (Dust in the back of the throat) a disposal of morality, a placing under the chair of more than the duck-billed hat, the denim legs planted wide.

Drinking. All those stories you might have missed/all those stories you might have heard. To imbibe or not: depends on the side of the story.

So the dust that lays itself down on the main street of Edberg is doggish, watchful rather than serene. An uneasy village, knowing it will never be a town, every new building balanced by another burned down or hauled away, every old building tottering into decline, although the screened-in porches of the early houses still dream shady afternoons in the scent of caragana and lilac. Positioned poor relation to Camrose, Camrose swallowing the farmers' equipment and grocery money, even their children's schooling, just up the Aberhart Road. You thought Aberhart lived on that road, owned it. Don't even know if you ever heard of the real Aberhart, or if you were just old enough for Manning doubting the future on CFCW.

In such uneasy souviences, do you remember or forget? Or is it all an elaborate fabrication, the village of Edberg and the farm two miles south and two miles east part of a puppeteer's gesture pulling the strings of source? Even on arrival, you are scouting out a grave. It still seems endless: Edberg. Without a time limit or the decency to know when to efface itself. Worse, it claims you, insists on a reference, influence, empreinte.

Impossible: somewhere to come from/never to run away to.

Initiation coppice.

TRAINING

The train went through. Even stopped (for a while regularly) when the station was manned and the creamery shipped. In the foreshortened sound of deep winter, its crossing wail reached the farm, hung suspended in the cold's throb. A ten-after-seven clock, a ten-to-eleven clock, although it was at night it sounded/ at night when you heard its clicking rush two miles away. Giving

Edberg self-importance: a schedule, a reminder. (The outside world, north, south, passing through/interrupting itself for Edberg.)

The stationhouse royally situated beside the track, a bit off from town (as if importantly, a self-deception), and the station-master too, with his cap and his watch chain, deciphering the argot of the telegraph stutter. The platform stood on the lip of the world, and if you could manage to ignore the cream cans and tractor parts, the wooden baggage cart, you could imagine (an Anna in black velvet stepping down to take a breath of air on her way to one of the family estates: it is the Edberg platform that nudged and gestured, peering and curious) the platform a promenade, it was that even and level and inspiring.

And even the diminishing waiting room with its pot-bellied stove could not dispel the seriousness of the train's potential destinations: the bench for waiting was wooden and pewlike, a furniture of gravity.

It might have been a guide for how to get there (away).

Although the stationmasters were assorted, and the station-house, though it seemed grand to you, poorly insulated, freezing in the winter and boiling in the summer, and although it had a curving (oak) staircase leading to the forbidden upstairs, the stationmaster's wife cut hair and did perms in the kitchen, amidst the potato peelings and the piles of washing.

She gave you your first (real) haircut, a damp roly-poly woman whose apron cut into her stomach and who seemed to wear a perpetual chuckle creased on her chin, it was cut like a bowl from your forehead down around your ears, and you remember tossing your suddenly lightened head, the lovely straight shake of hair with the tangled ends gone, swept into her red-rosed dustp(l)an. The kitchen door that her hair customers used faced the main street of town; the important side of station and track and ticket wicket and platform and waiting room and freight office, and down along the rails the elevators (was hidden).

Was the station first or last on trips to town? The short curved drive barely gravelled, grass growing in the middle of the track, easily snowed under, the perfect place to get stuck in snow or mud (because the railway company was too cheap to gravel it) three seasons out of four. It must have been first: dropping off the crates of eggs or the heavily cool cream cans in time for the dayliner's schedule before the round of other errands: hardware/ garage/grocery/post office: revolving the train, its warning whistle from the level crossing north and then the grinding brakes as it pulled itself (arthritically/theatrically) to a stop.

Level crossings with their own recitation and inflection: trucks, cars, motorcycles, wagons. Death by level crossing: even if the engineer saw you it was probably too late for him to try to stop, and although they blew and blew (the whistle), when the train hit, it hit, and bodies or the twisted metal flung itself into the air, the ditch beside the track, in a gesture of defeated dis-belief. Even with crossing lights and clanging bells, people were still hit (crossing). Death by level crossing a favourite choice for departures (whether deaf or drunk or forgetful).

There couldn't have been that many: (you start counting, on your fingers) or were there? Does it only seem as if the accidental visitation of the train was so common (never usual or ordinary, not an expected death, but common). Forgot to look/ forgot the usual time/didn't hear/tried to beat it: all coronary speculations, since the outcome was inevitably final. The fourteen-year-old on the motorcycle, the old man in the grain truck, the woman going home from the curling rink. Implacable training for departure.

You crossed that track every day twice for your entire school-going life. The bus driver (gum and candy at Christmas, the horn honking when you were late) always stopped, opened the passenger door and listened to the silent hum of silence. Ghost train, you suspect it hurtled itself down that run from Edmonton to Drumheller when nobody was looking or riding, on the rampage (the dayliner). Smelling of bananas and cigarettes, its slippery seats welded to the floor, the windows sooty.

Cancelled, stamped extinct now, although there is the fiction of an excursion train from Edberg to points south (once a week), just as you recited the fiction of the Duhamel (longest wooden trestle in the world) Grand Trunk Pacific bridge across the Battle River coulee, subsequently torn down, and only an image in the unremembered imagination (except for the wooden joists still faintly imprinting the bank where its great curve slumbered).

How many farewells/deaths/welcomes/shopping trips did that train's platform launch; or abortions/abandonments/divorces? The silent unmentionables never confessed to but capable of leaking their way through town, between one house and another, down the road to the nearest farm, and inching over the party lines to further districts. Taking the train was a statement: an entrance or an exit on the stage of Edberg.

You picked up your first boy on that dayliner (going to

Edmonton to visit your brother – were you even fourteen?). It was easy. Despite the conductor, his sharp-creased uniform wielding his little puncher. But you never had a chance to do much more on that train (except maybe fall asleep) re/turning home from Edmonton/university. Except stare out the window through the Battle River valley and the impossibly fairy-tale dense trees south of Camrose and across the bridge before racketting through the junction and sliding up to Edberg from the northwest.

No town without a train/no train without a town.

In its six square blocks difficult to establish main street, although you suppose it is the street that drives itself through, the street strung with year-round Christmas lights. The village itself strung along that gravel intersection: the school/houses/ Erickson's store/a blank-faced building? shed?/the hotel/another dusty storefront with a tabby sleeping in its window/the Co-op store/across the street Nick Radomsky's hardware and the garage/around the corner the coffee shop and the fire hall and the village office and the post office/more houses/more houses.

But nothing more than decreed (with houses hunched between, abashed, ungrand), curiously few trees along the picket fences, the splitting sidewalks. The road's dust haloing everything.

And by the track the stationhouse, elevators looming around the long curve. The elevators a repeated compilation of patience in the truck cab while your father delivered grain, drank coffee with Don Scott in the office, surrounded you are now certain (your memory insists on metal tags and wooden cubbyholes, the grassed ramp leading up to the oversize door and the giant's scale) by Elephant Brand signs. The open ladderlike stairs, the grind of cables and pulleys, the dust. Elevator men (Scott and Hashiuk – there must have been more, or others?) engraved on that patience.

Dust over all. A dead town: Edberg.

And yet, a knot of buildings together murders its own justification. A town (well, a village really) exists. A place, though far from Ellesmere, though not so large or portentous as an island, though not so essential that it is named on every road map, although a few acknowledge, a few cite faithfully.

What justifies place? The railway making the Battle River valley and its watershed accessible? The instigators? The Battle (or Fighting) River itself, drawing its lazy line through a crossing and un/crossing of: Indians/saskatoon berries/fish (jackfish and suckers)/coyotes. Henday (1754): Thompson (1787): Fidler (1792): Henry (1810): their wandering bivouacs.

The flats of Dried Meat Lake "studded with groves of ash-leaved maples many of which are a foot in diameter" (Macoun, 1879); "the fertility of the Battle River district" (Deville, 1883); "partly wooded and with scattered trees and coppice" (Tyrrell, 1887).

Dream yourself a place: Edberg.

Who's to blame: the Scandinavians who started the place? John Edstrom, bringing his coffee with him from Dakota, and his naming. Swedes and Norwegians by way of Minnesota and the Dakotas and Washington. Bredeson and Olufson, Johnson and Graham and Jensen and Berglund and Olson and Ramstad and

Young and Hansen and Olstad and Torhjelm.

Who started it: the water tower leaning a little on the berg, the short hill behind the church (a Lutheran church of course), the Elks Hall? What came first: a store, a mail station, a black-smith? Or was it simply where the wagons stopped.

The Scandinavians: ate smelly fish at Christmas and their mothers doubled as ballplayers and cakebakers. Heather Graham's mother made birthday cake with money in it, the dimes and nickels wrapped in waxed paper in the angel food, and there were always new kittens in the barn and the playhouse behind the clothesline and the raspberry canes you were supposed to stay out of but never did. Hiding in order not to have to go home, your mother's note getting that streak of impatience, sick of yelling for you to come because she was leaving and she was leaving you behind. They had TV, although you never watched, instead played upstairs in all the closets. You knew that house as well as your own, can remember the exact placement of the furniture in each room, the hardwood floor in the living room with its unused front door, the large metal kitchen table. The little drop-leaf egg table that you have now, that your mother bought for you at the auction the two of you sat underneath, drawing large characters, As and Es, with crayon. You can read it still if you bend your head under its leaves. Writing place: hiding place.

Swedes and Norwegians: settling Edberg. There for ages, before anyone, grandfathers before, owned your farm before you owned it, coming back unable to find it, so unrecognizably changed.

The namings of childhood: Boden and Brockhoff and Snider and Egert. Germanick and Cowan, Sand and Westfall, Johnson and Johnson and Johnson. West and Henderson and Rolseth and Falk. Hiving an Edberg. Mixes and cousins and second cousins, and family dis/cousins, related and ir/related and inter/related. Brothers and aunts, in the strange dance of settlement: "related or not, I'm coming!"

You weren't related to anyone: except your three brothers and your sister. That was plenty. And as for Dutch names, van Herk was the only one: still is/still there/still Dutch. Too bad, you always wanted to be a Sharp or a Smith, a Brown or a Buch.

Edberg: *Deadberg* (the other schools chanted at the ball tournaments). The road to there is paved with old intentions, farm boys in pickups, telephone wires, the dart of gophers. Gravel pinging the bottom of the car, dust behind and behind, a long shadow.

Edberg: a small town, you say, offering origins, the true Albertan's pedigree of place: curling bonspiels and ball tournaments, with Saturday night dances and a jukebox in the café.

Hell: not quite so arid as Sinclair Ross' Horizon or Robert Kroetsch's Big Indian/not quite so far away from Ellesmere.

Heaven: a sleepy street below cotton clouds; a general store with candy in glass jars and a Black Cat sign in the window; a post office with a wooden wicket that clattered open on newspapers and stamps; a school where the nineteen kids who started grade one together graduated together twelve years later in a mutual exercise of perseverance.

Whose portrait is this?

Too good to be true/too bad to be believed.

Only the train's daily engravement convinces you that you are ever going to get out of there, escape. Edberg an incentive to run away from home.

But what a place to grow up: no crime, no drugs, no raging hormones.

No, but the county cop from Bashaw swaggered over to investigate who broke into the Kotex machine in the girls' washroom and stole the money; in the exit doors of the school (or over on the sports grounds) you smoked through recess and noon hours, hid your cigarettes in your lunch pails; behind the curling rink you traded hormones for hands.

How to quit school: get knocked up: either knockee or knocker.

How to get away: get your license: drive fast on loose gravel: play chicken.

How to get laid: import a girl (or boy) from Bawlf or Rosalind.

How to get drunk: behind the school, behind the hall, in the back seats of cars, at the ball diamond, behind the curling rink, behind the elevators, down by the Battle River bridge.

Drink and get laid and get away and quit school.

Quit school and get away and get laid and get drunk.

Reverse all orders: this is as far as you can get from home. This is place, inescapable. This is as far as you can get. The train leaves and doesn't return.

ALLOWANCES

What you weren't. Allowed.

: to go uptown at noon. Either to the store, the post office, the café, someone's house. All potential trouble. Candy and chips in the store, loitering in the post office, the basement in someone else's house, the jukebox in the café, cigarettes everywhere, not to mention makeup and sex. All potential trouble. You were supposed/expected to stay in school, play on the swings, in the gym, read a book, do homework. Between the desks an illusory safety, the classroom aisles had just as many initiations and bloodlettings as the streets uptown. At noon you trembled with energy, needing to turn Del Shannon up loud in the café, drink coke, suck cigarettes from each other's fingers. You read it as strangely tame now. But the miracle of danger rotates from its source, not itself. As dangerous for you to sneak uptown as for a kid now to rob a bank.

: to play ball after school. Base/ball diamonds were suspect, between the catcher's mitt and the pitcher's mound anything could flash past/get loose/be taken. After school the teachers dribbled home, what did they care what game you played. Basket/ball winter's game, the court echoed with repeats, the stage in the gym had curtains that closed. And there were tumbling mats, beautifully stacked to soften floors, the space under the stage a dark warren of chairs. Foot/ball required taking the bus or a car somewhere else, and that was for boys, the girls only along for the ride/cheerleaders/providers of liniment. Curling bonspiels just used rocks instead of balls, and they went on all night, later and later as the winners won. Ball/games were time bombs.

: to ride in a car with anyone other than an adult older than thirty. Which may explain why you were forbidden to play ball/or your being forbidden to play ball may explain why you were not allowed to ride in cars with anyone other than an adult older than thirty. Or drive yourself. Which is what incited you to make up for this loss, your white Porsche a double driving: flaunting and denial, although it would take some genuine contortions to do anything in those snug bucket seats. Besides, you are older and your knees do not bend so easily as they might have then. (Still, you hiked up your skirts to show them, your knees. They were damn good knees.) But cars were sites for potential danger: where you were killed, or where you got knocked up, or where you got drunk: transportable sites of sin and transgression with doors that could lock, engines, heaters, back seats.

: to go to dances. A multiple grief of denyings. You wanted to dance: you still love dancing, you are and will always be a passionate dancer. Danced to the radio as far back as you can remember, danced when you should have been pretending not to, danced while you were reading, read while you were dancing. But dances were not dangerous for dancing: they were dangerous because they were in the Elks Hall and because people went to them in cars with back seats and in the middle of the dances went outside for a drink, and bang, you were knocked up. You were not allowed to go to dances because it was a sure thing that you would be instantly knocked up. Who would do the knocking and whether you would permit yourself to be a knockee was irrelevant. Going to dances had only one outcome. Can you refuse to dance? can you fall in love dancing? can you dance your way out of love? You went to a dance in the Elks Hall in Edberg only a few years ago and you were surprised at how staid it decanted itself, how careful, how cautiously polite, when you had been led to expect such wild revelry/such drunken staggerings/such furtive gropings of instant hands and bodies in the long grass beside the building, all of your fiction etched to a never readable page. Saved from your own story.

: to smoke, drink, or screw (in any guise under any circumstances); swear too (although that could always be done under your breath). You deliberately tried them all. Not screwing, nobody you wanted to do it with badly enough, figured it was smart to wait until you hit the big city and found somebody with experience, a likely potential for improvement, a trained professional. The furtive gropings of Edberg boys were dangerously innocent. Boyfriends came from Heisler or New Norway; if you were really lucky, Camrose or Bashaw. Seduction from a distance, the unknown stranger, not the cow-licked grin sitting across from you since grade two, no way to make romantic those gangly arms, those bitten fingernails.

: to fail. This was the only easy interdiction. You couldn't have failed if your life depended on it, school was too easy and you had figured out the mechanics/rituals of giving the right answers to assignments/tests/questions so early you could have composed them all (assignments/tests/questions). Just never let on you knew more than the teachers did: it pissed them truly off, these smart-ass immigrant kids reading more than they were supposed to know how to read.

Edberg: the place of varying allowances/forbiddences.

The Mennonite kids were forbidden more than you were, thank god. They were forbidden to wear pants (the girls), to have their pictures taken, to listen to the radio. They could not cut their hair or wear miniskirts, and as for getting knocked up, boys and girls weren't even allowed to sit on the same side of the church. No chance for a furtive tickle, a quick caress.

Who allows/forbids what? And where did the Mennonites come from? They simply appeared, the first ones moving onto the Hansen place next door (when the Hansens sold out and moved to Camrose), the huge old house sheltered between the spruce trees, and then more and more: Boese and Friesen and Isaac and Baerg and Megli. Kids and more kids, the girls with their tight braids bouncing against their backs and the boys with their suspendered pants. An edge of vernacular to their speech that erected an instant ridge, the inflection of otherment, language not quite so easily inhabited. An anabaptist influx tugging Edberg in another direction, thundering up the dusty road toward a place lost to its intent, another religion to compete with the Lutherans and the Baptists and the long-lost heathen. They built a church just past the railway tracks at the corner, two miles south of town: edged onto the village a new gesture.

Allowances: forbiddences.

Your parents thought that summer Bible school would be good for you/you couldn't get too much of a good thing. There were no Calvinists around so they sent you to both the Lutherans and the Mennonites (did one counteract the other, religious vaccination?). The Lutherans were easy going, taught cordial human relations, kindness to your neighbours and the world (red and yellow, black and white). In the Lutheran church basement on the hill above Meeting Creek you made buildings with popsicle sticks, you glued together stories with construction paper. Damnation/salvation mostly ignored. At noon you ate outside, picked saskatoons, played tag around the lilac hedges surrounding the church. On the way home the adults (Lutheran) driving you dipped into Meeting Creek (its breathless valley) to stop for popsicles.

The Mennonites made you nervous. Their slightly musty smell in the church, an unplaceable odour of repression. You learned more Bible verses and did fewer crafts; talked less and listened more; thought less and memorized instead. The Mennonite kids called all the adults by their first names in a strange parody of intimacy, you had been trained (European tradition) to address people properly, as Mr. and Mrs. Their lunches strange to you: cold tea and blood sausage, curdish cake that made you gag. And a Biblically sexual edge to everything you could see and sense, as if effacement only heightened its presence; repression made it stronger. The long-lost heathen of Edberg had nothing on the potential (if restrained) sexual transgressions of the Mennonites (even an eyelash can be sinful when censored). Innocence becomes its own corruption. You could not place this emanation but it lingered, identifiable, like taste. And you tasted yourself outsider/forbidden in some subtle way (although you were included, treated courteously, tolerated as a child of the community): a withholding, an inflection of distance that resisted acceptance. You know it now for that everywhere similar and famously rigid Mennonite clannishness and censorship: a rigourous ignoring of your slender bare legs/short hair/short sleeves/wild eyes that read itself as tight-lipped downright devil-dipping disapproval. At noon you played prisoner's base or hide-and-seek behind the outdoor toilets (always toppled at Hallowe'en and somehow re-erected before the subsequent Sunday); but there was no animal freedom in the game.

Although the Mennonite kids had their own rebellions/fictions/their own approach to getting around forbiddences. They just didn't do it with you: separatist sinfulness.

Mennonites and Scandinavians: at odds, unmiscible.

How, then, do you occupy a place: a site effacing itself, a town dis/appearing, dis/allowed.

REMAINDERS

Edberg that place where awareness made itself known, not so much memory as consciousness that you took breath and had existence. The disappearing locations of appearances: sites of seeing. Escapation: occupation: sites of initiation and marking (the soul's tattoo).

Edberg a village left in the wake of passing, itself a vanish-ment of waiting. Which came first: the wagon trail? the people? the railroad? the longest wooden trestle bridge in the world? The model-A slumping into itself back in the tangled bush of the cow pasture once drove through Edberg, gaily, its horn thumping. The old hulk rustles with animals now, wheel-wells flaking into rust. It had a sun roof, left open, and the springs of its upholstery were firmly coiled, although the cloth and stuffing had been gnawed to tufting. One old touring car: reading the wake of a passing people: a site effaced.

The cart trail itself: a scant etching through the bush, vanishing past the fence line into Young's pasture.

The train: discontinued despite its momentous schedule, its deaths and carryings, its steady timing with mail and cream and eggs.

The stationmaster's house: abandoned: moved or burnt? Gone.

The creamery: crumbled and mouldered and then burnt too, the same creamery where your brother put the "wait in the car" in neutral and it started down the hill. He wanted to steer, but when you were rolling he was aimed at the ditch, and your mother came running out, ran beside the car to jump in and step on the brake, stop it.

The barbershop: the pool hall: together: a faint turning of coloured pole: an echo of cues, not even the green felt tables sitting fat-legged and promissory left.

The Chinese café: a long way back, on Christmas, the Chinaman alone/a single light burning in the back of the high-foreheaded store. Your brother asking him to come out, but his preferring to be alone, there with his single flame.

The town pump: a public water tap that sat in the middle of the town for anyone to use: the water splashing into clean cream cans and the strong arms of the farm women without wells lifting it into the backs of pickups, the trunks of cars, gossiping there beside the café: torn out, cemented over, its small grey utility building vanished.

The café: one of the last to stay/go: a curved glass front and the few tables in the window, the row of red leather and chrome spin seats where you played the jukebox (three songs for a quarter) and waited for fate to erase time, where you ate pop and chips and watched the road to see if anyone new would drive up (telephone linemen or travelling salesmen): where your mother bought you your first ice-cream cone (strawberry) for getting straight Hs in grade one, the beginning of tradition: you always got an ice-cream cone there (you didn't have a freezer at home) if you got high marks or won a prize (for penmanship) in the county fair.

The blacksmith shop: turned itself over on its own ashes, in the end a kind of messy garage run by a converted Mennonite.

The Health Clinic: where the long-needled nurse visitationed once a month, her pink sweater over her white starch no disguise: she was a mean one vaccinating a row of you (your arms held out to her like drumsticks) as if you were small animals (made Shirley Cowan cry): disappeared, sign and blue asphalt-sided building gone.

The teacherages: their coved roofs hiding narrow houses where the teachers lived their impossible lives (what did they do behind their doors? impossible to imagine them in the bathroom or hugging each other): remote from ordinariness, although you might have been tempted to heave a rock through a basement window: hauled away.

The bus garage: replaced by a new steel structure without the double mouth of doors, the weeds growing beside.

The hardware: its dusty scent of crockery and nails, appliances and paint, garden hoses: Nick's office at the back (upstairs: was there an upstairs?): its plate glass windows reflecting past the Co-op: burned down.

Erickson's Locker Plant: where you lingered to read the magazines: their shiny tarnish: thawed, altered for some other function.

The Co-op store: its wooden candy cases, its arrangements of scoop and string, brown paper and oiled floors: fixed up, cleaned up, modernized.

The hotel (with its secretive beer parlour): exactly the same (from the outside at least).

The post office: its wooden front, its sign, its postal code and flag: embarking messages to the world, letters waiting to arrive, the wall of metal boxes shining with their small-toothed locks (cubbyholes of expectation), Box 61, Edberg, Alberta: suddenly up and moved: across the street, a dis/location: mail moving.

And yet, the site persists, re/news its presences.

New, untarnished: the drop-in centre, the library, a dozen houses, the road's thin paving, the middle-aged shifted to old and the young shifted elsewhere. A bedroom community for dreaming, the initial idea of city.

The germ of origin, its coppice: toward the west/Alberta/ Canada/the world: Edberg dreams of other islands of dis/ location. An encroachment on silence, its waiting for the stagecoach/the wagon/the train/the car/the airplane: to carry it further, a seed locked in its wingpod.

Is this a place from which to launch a world, a river, or even a short story? Can it launch itself?

Glacial Lake Edmonton's overflow origins the Battle River, that lingering thread twisting itself through the compulsion of willow and poplar: a high, wild bank bearing the north wind. The Battle River a site for naming beyond Edberg. The Battle River a glacial snout where school picnics exploded themselves into the river hills: where the Rodeo still cries its fences: the gravel pit where the high school kids still go to drink and neck (serious stuff, no stopping at the belt, no hands-off territory of bra and panties): a bridge and fishing: the swallows eager hiving. The Battle River draining the south end of Dried Meat Lake below the lowering crouch of Dried Meat Hill where the Indians dried the sun into their buffalo meat. The Battle River endlessly escorting Edberg, pressed alongside, a loop silvering seasons.

Good people should stay here: at home. Invent Edberg as home, invent a home for it. Send it to a retirement home for villages, washed up, settled out, even if the bulk gas station and the Co-op store are still open. String lights over the street at Christmas, invite a few dogs to keep watch. The farmers moved from the farm come down their steps mornings, dream their way to the post office, the drop-in centre. The farmers still hesitating on their land drive in and join them, between the coffee mugs they sigh to each other over another vanishment, speak of you gone into the maw of larger and larger cities, children taking strange trips to the north pole, trying to find Russia, and where will it all end? With murder? With a woman in a novel getting off a train in Edberg, her red bag in her hand, seeking to fulfil a fiction? Fictions that were opened even before Edberg was built, sawn and hammered into itself in the prairie sun by the Scandinavians and their practical sense of the necessary.

Living in town has much to recommend it: a watchfulness, an ease, children home from school at lunch blown along the street. The buses carry the farm children's ever-narrowing circles, the route a spider of rote over the years dragged into the school revised again: the old elementary with its staircases and home economics room torn down, salvaged, the brick high school become the elementary, but the ball grounds and the hollows worn smooth below the swings speak the same buzz of recess and noon to children fewer in number now, selected, grave.

Gravity at work: the motions of feet angling across the street a steady care, the hands sorting the mail from the flyers with serious intent. You try to hold it in your hands, Edberg, cup your hands to enclose this soft jumble of houses and streets, mangy dogs, the half-wit boy who sits eternally on the hotel steps, his sad head, his impossibly delicate feet. How to kindle between two palms the train's arrival and departure, the swell of Saturday night when stores stay open until eight and cars begin dusting in for the hall or the beer parlour. Marriages and funerals in-frequent in their strokes, so few babies now brought home from St. Mary's in Camrose.

Who's done it? Collapsed this careful edifice, this dreaming? The telephone? the car? the road? airplanes? weather? Can you permit it to remain upright (on its tired feet laced into farmer's boots), or will it fall flat onto its high-fronted face? Edberg imagining itself a presence, cleared its own stone-fields, its own edgy services.

And will it hang black crêpe over the same strings of Christmas lights before it dies: will it read past its own murder: un/read its eagerness to read the future: read its certain demise, its accidental blood and sweat.

Who comes from there carries in the hands (cupped hands leaking water or sand): no movie stars or singers: teachers, nurses, farmers, preachers, maybe a social worker, a dentist or two, one publisher, one writer. But escaping the cracked and leaky hills, the Battle's plunge, is impossible. The publisher drives home to remind himself of forgettings. The writer cries on the front porch she was never kissed on. What happened to you that you didn't stay? What happened that you failed to marry the boy/the girl next door and settle into your parents' occupation, drive into Edberg for the mail three times a week?

Edberg: what was missing there?

Culture? the annual variety night in the school gym with its songs and skits: the kid who fell off the stage and bloodied his nose, the kid who shocked her parents by singing out of clothes into a microphone. Baby grands and violins? There were piano lessons on the old upright in the Turner's house, the travelling piano teacher coming one day a week, next day on to Bashaw, then back through New Norway until the week swallowed itself to the next lesson. And you practiced on a pedal organ, trying to strike the keys as if they would respond like a piano.

Sport? the gladiator's heart? Ball games where Edberg was always beaten by Ferintosh, ball games where Edberg wiped New Norway, where Meeting Creek wiped everyone, ball games where what happened behind the backstop was more important than what happened in front, umpiric decisions made on or under wooden bleachers haunt you all: marriages and deaths, certainly the future of the catcher and the short stop.

Morticians, beauticians, electricians? You shape your back to anything if you have half a chance. Carpenters, mechanics, preachers? Who needs certification, schooling, when the hands can carry out the task? Bookstores and whorehouses, universities and banks. Edberg contains them all, a waiting behind the eyes, a reading of incentive.

Come back.

Everywhere is here. Your frozen dreams from the time when you stepped neatly down this sidewalk, your itchy palms from longing to be touched, your un/read stories. Edberg is an Ellesmere, an island shrouded in the wet snow of summer, with muskoxen waiting for their coats to grow. A movie un/made, with the auctioneer and piemaker as heroes. A bar fight holding on until Saturday night when the bodies will roll and flail down the splintered stairs and fenders will duck from one another in an insubstantial moonlight. Down the valley the Battle River will overflow, seed babies, break arms, drink rye and ginger. The cars at the gravel pit will play chicken with their sobriety. Teenagers will get on the train/get on the train/get on the train: the train will appear out of the dusk, snow-muffled cleft of the Battle River, and Anna Karenina will get off to pace the platform for a few moments, just long enough to see Tolstoy's coachman and to remember that illegitimacy lurks everywhere, she has only to read the story differently, her own story waiting to be un/read by the light of these places: all places with acts of reading as their histories, and all of them your homes. Edberg has carved itself into the cleft above your mouth. Your nose has an Edberg slope to it, your eyes Edberg's hills. This is your self-geography, the way you were discovered/uncovered in Edberg's reading of your fiction.

And how to unearth the place in the person? These six square blocks: this village barely villaging itself on this brief hillside of parkland, suggesting only other places: the church spire pointing to heaven: the crossroad pointing north and south and east and west (everywhere but here): the hall pointing below. In the basement of the person rests the village of Edberg, refusing to be dislodged, a continuous grounding.

Dust through it yourself, then. Check out the landmarks and see if your reading has been just. A few curtains will flick aside; the beer in the parlour is cold enough; hot coffee in the drop-in centre; stamps in the post office. If you stop at the school the kids will form a circle and stare, you seem so ancient in your telling: they have read you (your younger pictured face on the wall) and forgotten in their own un/reading of this world. Their parents were your peers: your friends and enemies, demanding and enlarged between bloody noses and birthday parties and the long, jouncing bus rides home. The buildings are so certain of themselves they all act nameless, although the streets have been assigned.

You cup your hands to hold it in, breathe deep. You want to command it into everlasting place like a horse or a dog, a patient animal. You look away: it moves, un/reads itself again, a sly alteration leaving you puzzled and groping for reassurement. You check with other originals, try to compare your grainy photographs with theirs (Joyce Brockhoff, Julia Siemens, Dennis Johnson, Heather Graham). Impossible: their versions negate yours. You drink each other under the table in an effort to remember your own awkwardness and the others' menace: the way they scared the hell out of you then, the way everyone in that place scared the hell out of you, they were all so much more knowing: good preparation for leaving and how if only you'd had that chance to dance you might have carved yourself a small ungainly niche in which to remember and forget. Some of them have pasts you'd like, living there and coming back so easily, as if Edberg were a place to return to, happily retrieved.

Or all the ones who stayed and married each other, who get together for barbecues and pot lucks, who make sure their kids don't fight, who stayed and stayed, who stay. Who look at you suspiciously, your name a flag for caution. You could be dangerous to the peace of the place: the piece you carried away is up to you. They read your lips, your clothes, your foreign car, your absent husbands. The extended hand is tentative: you might read scars they don't want printed or revealed. You ache to reassure them you are only looking, wanting to un/read Edberg (in its daily habits) as badly as they do. Sniff and edge, those are the marks of reunion. Un/reading: de/coding: what lives behind the passing clock? Whose child is whose, and where do you live now?

Here, still, forever, camped on the edge of the graveyard so gravely sited above the Battle River. Hanging there, once rawly new, its fence fiercely civilized. Until you started filling its space: children dying in the arms of time, adults switching allegiances from breath to silence. The Edberg graveyard as an end, a shift in being. A place to stay, settle down, send roots. There is seldom mist here on this grey promontory, just clear moonlight. The coyotes howl along its caraganaed edge, the long grass bends unmowed. You dream your own stone there: its site: a carved tombstone that knows eighteen years of longer living than any other place: the city of graves enough to be a place itself. An island in the world: an arctic metaphor for escapation.

Come back. Come back.

Return: escape to embarkation/escapation. The shabby little town, moored so steadily in its thirties style, slowly subsides. The model-A moulders into the ground beside you, the Mennonites and Scandinavians at last lie quietly together and there is dancing between the graves, all of you finally dancing: and the ground cover shifts with the celebrating bodies in their hot joining below.

Edberg has already sidled past the edge of your vision, down a side alley and away. Country urban: prairie town. A coyote slinking along the too-populous section lines, tail down and muzzle hesitant. A porcupine, lumbering into coppice. Retiring, ready to lapse quietly into the deep breathing of forget.

All those boys you might have kissed, the dawns you would have waited up for, the girls you would have traded secrets with. Missing: unread. Waiting to be discovered in the books you carry when you travel to exotic islands. Written into place, this edgy village, this tormented street wishing you were a Faulkner and it were able to hang on (to you) for a few decades more.

Edberg goes on with its falling, one molecule at a time: and you too in your ache to archive it there to read/remember/blame. To unhinge, and to carve with words. A reading act: this place of origins, of forbiddens and transgressions, of absence and remains.

Come back. There was a village here once, with a few stores and services, a handful of houses, a school. It rested and stays, still alters itself according to the need. When there are no more horses, the blacksmith goes; when there are no more children, the school goes; when there are no more letters, the post office goes. Where's the unreading here? Just practicality, necessity, the plowing of a people around their sloughs.

But Lundstrom's slough to the west of town reads more than that: still crackles the fall, ducks and the capped hunters down from the city for sport, the rattle of the car's steering as you follow the wheel around its long curve, the almost-appearance of Edberg over the rise: a signature of cat-tail and blue, of spring flooding or winter ice. Named: it shrinks and grows in wet years or in dry.

Edberg: this place, this village and its environs. A fiction of geography/geography of fiction: coming together in people and landscape and the harboured designations of fickle memory. Invented: textual: un/read: the hieroglyphic secrets of the past. Come home.

Enough's enough. Come home.

N

EXPLORATION SITE : EDMONTON

N

EDMONTON, long division

The North Saskatchewan cutting the town in half: north/ south; business/pleasure; government/learning. The few bridges incidental to separation and the high brows of the river banking their own domain. Here is the city that will divide you from the country, that will wean you from Edberg, its wide streets and narrow alleys leading toward seduction. This is the quandary you face, your problem in long division: north/south.

And what's to be expected of a fort(ress) set up to trade/skin Indians. The Hudson's Bay Company holding its own centuries later, Edmonton House but one dot of many stringing the North Saskatchewan, so long under the tyrannical eye of John Rowand ("We know only two powers – God and the Company!"), Chief Factor (1823-1854) whose bones were boiled to make his bread, still haunting the upper reaches of the north bank, where the Château Lacombe and Edmonton House turn themselves round. You can see him at dusk strutting his girth above the city he thinks he invented, the flats below him remodelling their green gardens.

You know Paul Kane's story of Christmas dinner in Edmonton (1847), with its dried moose noses, feasting and plenty and the dancing that stormed its steps through the endless night, and you imagine you too will feast after your long forbidding, after your incestuous waiting to be free to taste those delicacies, those impossible erotics never found in Edberg, only dreamed about listening to the radio in the late bloom of summer, the voice of the DJ in its husky promisement.

If you can only get to Edmonton in one piece, you now the Indian coming with your skin, your fresh eyes up from the Battle River country, through the Gwynne Outwash Channel, looking for a trade, something of use in the long winter ahead.

Long division: what you were never good at, had to concentrate for, practice. What choices are there? You set up the equation, begin with a thick-stemmed landlady who rustles through your closets when you are in classes, who insists you are amoral because you resist falling in love: not yet, not just yet. This city caught in its own nebulous prairie history: a fort(ress) to be stormed. Love must subtract a difference.

Edmonton: here the world rests outside the glass of cold, winter speculations.

CITY OF EDMONTON

situated at the head of navigation on the North Saskatchewan River; the centre of the Gold, Coal, Timber and Mineral region of the Great North-West, and surrounded by the richest wheat-producing country in the world.

The four great highways leading from Winnipeg, the great Bow River grazing country, the Peace River country and British Columbia via the Jasper Pass, centre on the Town Site.

It is the terminus of the CP telegraph line, the North-West mail route, and the projected Saskatchewan branch of the CPR.

The Hudson's Bay Co. offer for sale 1,000 lots on the above town site at low prices and on reasonable terms. All information can be had by applying at the HB Co. offices in Winnipeg or Montréal,

| R. McGinn, | C. J. Brydges, |
| Agent, Edmonton | Commissioner |

Just what you need, in 1882, a bare ninety years before your arrival, not entirely accurate in its projections but close, close enough. Although the CPR line went south to Calgary, and gold was in the eye of the beholder, the telegraph line was real enough, encoding Methodists and temperatures, local threshings and silver foxes. Toronto is full of expelled Jesuits and stern-chinned Presbyterians; landslides and murders the same as everywhere. You might as well start here.

How do you start a life in Edmonton? You buy a frying pan, a kettle, a teapot. Two bowls, two cups, two plates, a knife, a fork. Some towels. You lay the clothes you sewed out in your drawers, hang your dresses in your closet. They seem frumpy, not quite up-to-date. Is there any store (beyond the HBC) in which to purchase future? If Frank Oliver's were still going you could search there for the answer to your long division.

> (fourth door east of Methodist Church) has on hand a full stock of GROCERIES, comprising Black and Green Teas, Crushed Sugar, Coffee, Myrtle Navy Tobacco, Raisins, Currents, Rice, Oatmeal; Beans, Dried and Evaporated Apples, California Fruit, etc.; HARDWARE, comprising Grain Shovels, Miner's Shovels, Hay and Manure Forks, Ox Bows and Yoke Staples, Strap Hinges, Gold Pans, Quicksilver, 3-4, 5-8 and 3-8, Manger Rope, Canadian Axes and Handles, Large Mirror, Butter Bowls, Bread Pans, Ready-Made Stove Pipe and Elbows, etc.; BOOTS & SHOES, Men's and Women's Wear; and DRY GOODS, comprising Seamless Bags, and a few pair of extra good Overalls, Shirts, Drawers and Socks.

You need a large mirror, manger rope, crushed sugar, a gold pan, quicksilver. You will need to learn to play pool, to read in the dark, to elope.

You want to fall in love with a racer, a man with his hands

firmly on the reins, Jim Campbell with his highstepper challeng-
ing any horse within fifty miles. You need a horse: the walk to
university is long division itself, and the walk between the buildings, from class to class, a disorienting race, despite maps and
registration schedules, despite Tuberculin Tests and Library
Instruction. You try to pace days, promise yourself you will sink
in, settle down, but the autumn is impossibly crisp, and you feel
yourself staggering between adjustment and desire.

Why go to Edmonton if not to fall in love?

You do fall in love, with the thin insect legs of entomology,
with the zealous musings of philosophy, the incessant novels of
literature, the moustache of Maurice Legris as he chews you
through *Huckleberry Finn* and *Portrait of the Artist*. If lovers
cannot be found in Edmonton, they can be founds in books. But
where are the dances, the marriages, the murder trials? In hiding,
in retrospect.

You blur from one class to the next, one antecedent to
another. You need to be ferried from the south to the north side,
the city still un/read as you evade its gold/coal/timber mines and
dream of reading secret dyings. You have left your Edberg
murders behind and although red roses walk to your door, you
guard your own bank account and find a forester. Races and
footraces, elopements and amputations, will succeed. 11438-79
Avenue. The room overlooking the back alley and the garage still
suggests occupation, but the landlady is surely vanished with her
amputations of tenants and rules, her shrill commands while
poor-relation Anna did the bent-head and lifeless-eyes work. The
last time you avoided the landlady she had pitilessly stroked
herself into the hospital. Probably better than what you stroked
yourself into?

Here in this archaic, bottomed-out glacial lake, the bowl of city held in the hand of geological (10 000 years) time, only the river's incisement to remember division over melting. Legal fences and dis/legal fires incite rebellions, women are at a premium and should be allowed free, the turning of leaves into their own crumbling lights, the late afternoons of the city's burn when you walk heavy-footed home with your books and your bag of solitary groceries. You live on toast and tea; you want to go dancing; you slog through classes, papers (on Body Language, on Mark Twain, on existentialism, on the mandibles of grasshoppers); the heads of the young men all bent quietly away. The engineer in Philosophy class, the would-be singer and road construction worker in English with his November 9th Bastille day stormings of the body. Phone numbers etched in memory (465-6327, 429-8749) although estranged now, have changed owners, succumbed to answering machines and the ravages of push-tone dialling.

Long division: attainable in this outwash city overlooking its own autumns. Your landlady accuses that you work too hard, you read too much: she knocks on your door at all hours seeking to distract you (she teaches you to despise distraction), while you only want to return to words, the neat enlistments of notes, the swollen pages of portentous papers. Edmonton is a reading, an act of text, an open book. Beyond the door it crouches in lanes of leaves, and walking through its crackle you dream fire, river water, frozen breath, summerfallow, never suspicioning that you will turn south, eventually, to the beautifully groomed cemetery lawns of Calgary.

There are no silk handkerchiefs to steal, the insane are kept out of the city, heart attacks rage. You encircle books in your arms, a lovering persistent, although your purse has no revenue, your future has no kiss. But you remember every movie you saw: *Junior Bonner*, *Alice's Restaurant*, *Gone With the Wind*, *On the Buses*, *The Last Waltz*, *Pete and Tillie*, *Slaughterhouse Five*, *Love Story*, *The Last Picture Show*, *Fiddler on the Roof*, *Ryan's Daughter*, *Man of La Mancha*, *Travels with My Aunt*, *The Godfather*, *The Effect of Gamma Rays on the Man-in-the-Moon Marigolds*, *Brother Sun, Sister Moon*, *Jesus Christ Superstar*, *A Clockwork Orange*, *Class of '44*, *The Emigrants*, the dreaming screen.

Long division: pay up. Prospects superior, as long as you keep company with books. The Northcote might ply, winter might never arrive. Temperatures and ice thicknesses no longer measured, but winter comes nevertheless and your coat hopelessly inadequate, your legs always cold. Over-heated buildings flush the blood while the pages still insist on turning themselves over and over in the crowded and hustling library, the studious bent studiously and the restless restless. Rutherford is the wrong place for long division: potential for church but not passion. Starvation pay for love. You work at diminishing your innocence, you en/tangle yourself with students who seem unlikely to do more than turn pages.

And Russia is looming, luring, lurking, Anna's quick step on the platforms of desire reaches all the way to Edmonton.

> The Czar of Russia, who lost his wife a short time ago, is married again. He had not been blown up for several days and was feeling lonesome.

The world at large and Edmonton its stagnation point: how to get from this place farther, how to reach the reaches of the world, and maybe Russia. Are seductions to Arctic Islands possible? Do they read themselves a future, a presence on a map? You want to go there, Nova Zembla, its trembling promise, its unrailwayed joining.

> The Russian Government is trying to cause an emigration to Nova Zembla, an island within the Arctic Circle, by giving 350 roubles and five years' freedom from taxes to every able-bodied man who will emigrate there. They have a simpler and cheaper way of encouraging emigration to Siberia.

Bulletin opinion. The curved beauty of Nova Zembla drifts past the imaginations of Edmonton: long division.

Squatter's rights in Edmonton: the city waiting for you to unbend yourself in a basement room with a man who may or may not be worth unbending your good knees for. Who dares to fall in love with murderers at large? You go to more movies, you read more novels, your professor is astonished at what you remember from the bleached pages. Love does that; sexual attraction brings every hair to attention. You try to temper your initiations, but fall persists while the city dreams itself around you and the snow blots wet through your thin boots. Your coat is too short, your hair too unruly to be helpful, your hands red and chapped. Edmonton winters are not made for love or fondness, even for declarations or seductions. Outside the basement room, children shout as they run home through the snow, the school buzzer an echo of Edberg's, a start of guilt, of remindering.

Still, you've been abstemious enough, have yet to see the inside of a hotel, either historical or contemporary.

EDMONTON HOTEL
The Pioneer House of Entertainment West of Portage la Prairie
Pemmican and dried buffalo meat has long been a stranger at the

table, and its place has been taken by substantials more in keeping
with the onward march of civilization.

A cosy billiard room, where the Edmonton coal can be seen
burning to advantage.

Good stabling attached.

Donald Ross, Proprietor

Good stabling attached.

Long division: temperance. A new meaning to the old
missionary. These are the bars you drink at: the Corona, the
Riviera, the Park, the King Eddie, the Cap; the Embers, Ernie's.
A way of breaking free of books, sharpening your peripheral
vision, tensing your wrist muscles.

> It appears from exchanges that the name "coffin varnish," used at
> Edmonton last winter to denote a villainous compound swallowed by
> some of our thirsty fellow citizens for the purpose of producing a
> temporary exhiliaration, has travelled a long distance from home
> without having had its significance or usefulness impaired. It is now
> the popular name of the popular drink in Laramie, Wyoming, and
> various other classic localities. It is altogether appropriate that "coffin
> varnish" should be succeeded by "sudden death" which rejoices the
> hearts of the boys…

You drink: beer, Chanté Rose, Baby Duck, Sangre de Torro,
awful stuff. You survive a few hangovers, a couple of horror
shows, you enjoy a genuinely inebriate time (once or twice,
between implacable sobriety). But the grand division of sons of
temperance will call a convention in order to discuss whether the
time has not arrived to press for total prohibition. On all
passions.

You have not yet read *Anna Karenin*, but she is waiting to be
read, to remind you of what to expect of books, of love affairs

and their killings. It is reported that the Czar of Russia was assassinated. Still later it is reported that the czar is all right yet. Somewhere within the orbit of the Arctic Circle you deduce the potential of lost Shanghai pigs, of census takers as recording angels, of attacks of quinsey. You avoid the crime of deserting employment, of bones and tambourine, of eight-day clocks, which you are certainly circling. The czar is afraid to appear in public, even at religious ceremonies and the Herzegovinians are making it hot for their rulers.

Dances exert their magnetic field: their follow-up reports, bring their own applause:

> The Masonic ball on Tuesday evening last in McDougall's Hall was undoubtedly the best affair of the season...Not the least remarkable feature was the number of ladies – sixteen – the largest number that has been got together at any affair of the kind in Edmonton within the memory of man, or of which there is any authentic record. As our fashion reporter is away we are unable to speak critically of the toilets of the ladies or the costumes of the gentlemen, suffice it to say that although only one gentleman appeared in a clawhammer coat there was more lace, frilling, kid gloves, black cloth, starched linen and store clothes generally, not forgetting a few police uniforms, were at this ball than could have been collected in any previous year in the whole Saskatchewan country.

Sixteen ladies and a clawhammer coat. Keep a record of the ladies that come dancing. You wear short skirts, baggy checked pants, you buy a pink corduroy suit and a black blazer. But you always look slightly wrong, not quite as matched as the rich city girls who sit (Sociology) in front of you, whose neatly pressed flowered blouses vaunt cashmere cardigans, and whose perfectly straight teeth shine.

Through the maze of your books you try to read this place, this once-fort, Hudson's Bay Company stronghold, this ferried and rivered city. How to cross from one side to the other? The High Level trembles in the brisk north wind, its black lattice a crib of threat. From here the Mackenzie brigade went overland to Athabasca Landing and Fort Assiniboine on the Athabasca River. From here you will launch yourself north and west, south and east.

The street names (Jasper Avenue, McKay, Hardisty, Saskatchewan, Calgary, McLeod, Walsh) have altered themselves to numbers, but the ice in the river still grafts a thin skin in November, still grinds itself against the divided banks in an ecstatic breaking, an April canticle that springs winter free the same as it always did. Edmonton still a wooded valley up from White Mud Creek, Black Mud Creek, still the site of glacial long division, the self caught between origins and destinations: body and cemetery.

The cemetery question persists, demands consideration. High time the citizens of Edmonton arranged for a public cemetery. Delay causes increased trouble and expense: the long trek to bury outside the skirts of the city, the winter does not keep bodies nearly so well or so long, and death will proliferate, will insist. Edmonton funereal, where death is enacted but never finished. There are more ways to hang a cat than by choking it with butter.

But that high and hanging valley that traced you a faint outline for walking under the impossible brilliance of the northern lights still divides. The whole sky a vast teepee, the greater part white, but the lower portion towards the south and east a dark and spectacular red. If Calgary is famous for its endless and potent light, Edmonton is a city that you learned best through its darkness, never going to bed until dawn streaked five-thirty, and then sleeping through the day. Edmonton: still the darkness of winter and of buildings, of enclosed cold.

Despite passing, you spend a summer driving the tractor for your father, buy your own bed and find a landladyless apartment, erect shelves of bricks and boards, accelerate your reading. You avoid the football evenings with your classmates, you avoid the temptation to enter law, you avoid baking cookies into your professor's favour. While others divide and swyve, hunt life partners and missionary intent, you read, entext yourself a city of pages, their sybarite answers.

The jobs you take are yours, the hours you spend as typing temp for the government; ushering legs in the Paramount theatre (you saw *Butch Cassidy and the Sundance Kid* two hundred and forty times that summer, but it bought your wedding dress and a set of dishes); reading and marking for the blind professor of Religious Studies while around you engagements break and resettle, around you buzz LSATS and BEds after degree. The others seem to need no jobs, they go to church, have children and a social life, buy furnishings, while you turn desperate time to an eight-day clock on high speed reading. Six years engaged in long division, and without having ever put down your book, you are degreed, married, authored, even public and published, and out of there.

Swearing you will never return to your sites of seduction and rage, to the baffling problem of an eternal long division of the self, this Edmonton, still glazed with ice, pretends to be another place than it pretends to be.

You meet them now, Heidi (shy and still gap-toothed) at a reading in Spruce Grove, Len (who *did* work – in his father's bakery) suddenly around a corner in the stacks of MacKimmie, confiding alterations.

Dis/criminate these absent words: your brevities of Edmonton. Six years fore/shortened, refuse to be re/read. Conversion/metamorphosis/seduction. The criminal conversations of burial consigned to a potential desert woman, an island sublimination.

You visit Edmonton, longing for the foothills with their knowing cemeteries, their monuments to resurrection. Still you know, walking the quandam streets that walked you, here was long division and this the abacus.

N

Exploration Site : Calgary

N

∧

CALGARY, this growing graveyard

QUADRANT ONE : STONES

From within the grave you can only leave into light, burst through dark soil, arrival the admission of belonging: here/there/within. Or coming from.

Where is the world? "If everybody stayed at home, they would be good people" (Saint Joan via Shaw). So would she. You too. And helicopters remind you of the ground they settle on, the gerund they choose arriving or belonging, even leaving. Leaving becomes an act/ive grace, how it's done that is; belonging only a question of luck, ladies in high slippers doling out cards.

Why go away when everything is here? decremental: Canada, the west, prairie, Alberta, the south, Calgary: a house northwest, room, chair within the room, the molecules of breath (an address). Hemispheres and crumbling shores of rock name us a place to stay and hope it's there when we turn around, hope we're there when it turns around.

You learned one thing – settle under an escarpment, the omen of its shoulder nudging up the sky: you can afford to sleep at night, in the day sit tight under its shadow, safety in that wedge of neck. Found yourself a Jericho, have you? And the rest of the world has a sore throat. Lucky for you Joshua's moved east, he's whoring after strange places too (the temptations of exile). Keeps calling his travel agent and demanding another ticket. You don't know how he gets through customs. You can't, not without them tearing everything apart, accusing you of buying new shoes. Your theory is they don't have enough to do, they're so bored that even one planeload is a diversion. "Let's see how these guys pack" (on arrival).

Hermetics: the chambers of arrival. And when you finally hit the air, no choice but to be drunk on the altitude, that clichéd cerulean sky, P.K. Page's rarefied crystalline air. (She says it better than you do, but she doesn't have to live here.) Well, airports are graves, sounding chambers for the city as a unit of civilization. Despite the coyote chasing a rabbit across runways dodging jet-streams. Hah.

It's been said before: archaeologies are (in)formed by those who (in)vent them. Graves are for their visitors. Residents beware. And stones will work their way to the surface, no matter how buried and buried again. Rocks clattered onto the stoneboat hot August afternoons out in the summerfallow behind your father's and brothers' overalled legs, the little ones were yours while they levered the heavy ones with a crowbar. When you get old(er) you get to carry the crowbar. (You've got one now, in your garage, because it's a crowbar.) You carry stones home with you, the flutes of pebbles ground soft by tide, knife stones from the Indian quarry, you lie on your back to chip them from the roof. A small coffin that. The house is full of rocks shining in their corners. Enough to cover a grave, and heaped up too. Well yes, it's death that makes a place its own. A city is counted for the people who die there and who stay, are buried. There aren't enough graveyards here, people go away to die: their bones go elsewhere.

Calgary a silent freight train carrying away long rows of boxcars neatly stacked with coffins. Boxcars? How do bodies move? Plastic over a solemn grey coffin in the back of a Dan Dy Delivery pickup. A refrigerator car you suppose, but the CPR, the CPR, that's who does it, this is a CPR town, would've died otherwise. "The greatest transportation company the world has ever known" (E.A. Victor, Architect and Surveyor). The CPR rails reached the east banks of the Bow River on August 9, 1883. Forget freight rates, that's another story. (Don't get involved.)

But yes, a place is counted for the people buried there. Joyce (James) in Zurich perched neatly in brass, so much himself between the sorted and arranged, that formational Swiss cemetery. Giving the lie to Dublin, to Trieste. Waiting for pilgrims. No, not enough cemeteries here. Although there are G/R/A/V/E/S on the first map, 1883, right beside the RC Mission. (Section 10 just west of the Elbow, though later maps move the RCs east.) Graves elbowing each other awake, saying "move over." Marked on the maps an odd tinted green: Queens Park Cemetery, Burnsland Cemetery, Union Cemetery.

Cementery. Koimētērion.

Queens Park remote and placid above the city, highsticking its way through Cambrian Heights. Heights for the depths, crematoriumed over the spread city, those acres of rough prairie grass cut into hay mows, grass edging over the stones flattened against the ground, ears back, names disappearing into the foxtail and broom. Taken over, named effacement – gophers and rabbits alert and unrestricted, the acres and acres of henges stoning themselves up the hills (no, coulees).

Acres yes, fields, even sections: you got lost in the rows of upright headstones, thought you were going north when you were really going east, gravity does that to you, loss of orientation in the acres and acres rolling against Nose Creek there in the middle of split level bungalows the cemetery partakes of several coulees and a poplar bluff, acres and acres of prairie hay. Recorded history not in the austere and polite markers (granite, sandstone, marble, fieldstone) but the promise of names held and used and recorded: Tickler/Jealous/Kwong/ Dearness/Chan/Nowogrodski/Reizevort/Kiss/Bitonti/de Champlain/Stipic/Taylor/Evans/Fuchs/Zwir/Koo/Lightbody.

And the others, sliced by Macleod Trail pushing itself souther and souther, the rattle of motels and car wash gaseries, car lots and windowed food souther and souther even to the Ranchman's Bar smoky and rumbling pretending to cowboys ("Where the hell are we going?"), souther and souther. ("Are we in Lethbridge yet?") (Not yet Foth.) But yes, the city gets flatter and faster the souther and souther you go. You're driving over graves, that's when you know you're on the right trail, graves.

And the Chinese graveyard delicate and moving, its enigmatic calligraphy, Lee Yip (from Coaldale) all the homesick Chinese gathered into this bird's nest of eternal poise, all the homesick Chinese of southern Alberta buried high. And at night the tombstones (tablets) lean against each other in the eerie spool of headlights searching through their maze (templecular).

But despite acres and acres, there are not enough cemeteries here. In the phone book they are discreet, public and private, a short listing with numbers to call for information who will have numbers to call for a list of names, alphabetical and with location (Section One, Row M, plot eighteen). They are under the auspices of City Parks and Recreation, no pun intended. The private ones offer comforting names (Garden of Peace) (Memorial Gardens). As if it wasn't gardens that got you into trouble in the first place. Rows and rows, a garden (a place for growing). And no mention of graveyards, that repository of the poor, a blank space between gravel and greenhouse, though both might be appropriate, connected. Columbarium vaulting into heaven.

Of course, this is the sky of heaven, where it's kept in the meantime. And the wind makes this a dusty city, your archaeological longings flung into your eyes, induced tears.

Engravement then. The home of the spirit? To dare to stay here to die, to dare to stay after death, to implant yourself firmly and say, "Here I stay, let those who would look for a record come here." You want a death more exotic than it is, would choose repose in the arms of foreign grass, odd moles rather than gophers. But the lengths of darkness measured metre for metre are shorter here and the pinhole photography of death as immobilizing as east or west. The graveyards of Calgary are your grottos, and even ashes scattered and unburied settle here with the mosquitoes and the rippled gusts of wind off the foothills.

To belong then. Leaving not here but from here. Return implied. Sounding chambers for the city as a unit of civilization.

Enclosured, focussed, a possible fortress in walls and tombs. Choosing one or the other you stay. And in that staying you decide that home is here and death too is allowed.

You dare to be buried here, this Jericho revisited.

QUADRANT TWO : SOLVENCY

The declensions of Calgary insist on money, although money rejects declension (banking on itself, receivable).

Abattoirs and railway yards, oil offices (of course). Not derricks and pipelines but the bureaus, departments of and sections and divisions glued together in a scraper of intention, the crooked teeth of tilted buildings harbouring ambition, short-sightedness (Frac/tions). And money's occupations live their own short-lived lives.

Abattoirs have become Meatpackers and their offshoot markets, although Slaughter Houses are delicately mentioned and renamed. Beef Packers always specialists now generalized, but the stockyards, their high leathery smell all through the southeast (Burns Avenue, the first millionaire). Effaced into the Stock Exchange, small as it is. Still, despite unlisting, the stock yards retain their labyrinth, sprawl over their own railway mesh bawling and dusty, a swarm of Hereford backs on weekdays, buyers and auctioneers (many, many, as always) converging on the high-slatted trucks that roll in from the south and the east and the west.

Shoe leather. Tanneries have given way to tanning salons (despite 2207 hours of shine per year) and the hides of all the slaughtered animals are shipped away, east. Their bones ground fertilizer. A different coming to the garden, underground. Ho, although undertakers have become funeral directors (and a good many too), embalmers lost between elocution and embassies (not one). Shall we presume that there are none, that there is no money in the business (of death)?

But ah, blacksmiths there were (many) now only three, specializing in jackhammer points, then in horses. Horse Dealers then too (many) and still a few, but without the personality, the checked jacket and rakish cap, the trick with a foreleg and a burr. Who hung around the shooting gallery (one), now obscured behind some other muffled sound, distant boom still hangs in quiet evenings, despite the range, despite the earphones and the cardboard men. And Gun Shops thrive, their wares behind fly-blown windows (All Stories End).

Galleries are otherwise, under art, the two artists proudly listed in 1910 are commercial and designer now, and follow artificial limbs. Scenic artists vanished utterly, scenes too. And those cynical suspect a loss of purity, how barbers have become hair stylists and boot blacks shoe shine agencies, haberdashers lost themselves in department stores and hat reblockers (many) become the one hat renovator, who presumably rebuilds from the skull up.

Dressmakers have altered themselves to designers, clothiers, tailors and fashion consultants. And somehow you are certain this is no longer the safe occupation of mildewing maidens who stitch behind the safely drawn curtains waiting for spinsterhood to pass.

Although gloves and mittens are the same. So much for everyday.

So much for every day. Money talks.

What about the coffee roasters (machines instead of persons), the fire escape makers (completely lonely), Bible depots (proselytized), the mince meat manufacturers, the oyster dealers (prairie and pacific), piano polishers (with a soft cloth and a gleaming eye), Turkish baths, milk dealers? Dealers in – an interrupted need, the needing service changed. Who can say which comes first, money or the source. There will, it seems, always be a call for billiards and dentists and collection agencies. For interpreters and translators (although the one German translator in 1910 could hardly have credited the tongues unleashed now, would have opened an agency – gone crazy with delight in one word's inability to understand another).

There's money to be made. The new languages of the world call. And laundries do their best to keep you clean; nurses keep you well; wedding cakes persist. Annas tread their passions.

The quarries (two, of sandstone, long used up and closed) of money continue; and the once six surveyors have expanded all categories: Aerial, Alberta, Construction, Inertial, Marine, Offshore, Seismic. Surveyors and purveyors, a measuring and a counting, a weighing out.

As for pleasure, beyond the lost Turkish baths, the restaurants have always been Chinese; the theatres (the Dreamland, the Empire, the Lyric, the Orpheum, the Princess, the Starland) amalgamated filmic frames; the Orchestras and Bands (the Calgary Coloured Quartette) play on. Pleasure domes increase.

The boarding houses have all closed.

In this iconography of money, you are sharply divided. There are those who collect and those who will not, those who scorn to stoop for the quarter on the sidewalk and those who hoard, stuff mattresses (remember winter). There are seasons of money, houses bought and sold and never lived in, land surveyed into inches, buildings flooring themselves into Babel. Even when the cranes are abandoned and the vacant lots blow dust, the hoarding gaping and permanent, there is a season on money, that season when the secret hand writes a well-concealed cheque buying speculation and aspiration, banking on ugly phrases: real estate market, retail space, oil and gas futures, the property of mercy for lease.

Like death, money leaves, pretends it never lived here, and the rusty cranes and empty buildings fold and whisper on themselves, in the rustling silence of Calgary's own seduction and abandonment. What's to be expected whoring after strange futures? Still, beautiful enough for the next one to be caught, to hesitate and wager this or that against the lure of profit. Despite the office owners camped out on their unrented carpets, the bath shops-sold out of gold-plated faucets.

The declension of money is measurement. How much/how long/how old/how big? Your love of money is a frisson of pleasure to large-numbered years. The celebration of invented anniversaries. Economic intention signed, sealed, delivered. Struck a deal. All those Americans. Peter Prince and the Eau Claire and Bow River Lumber Company (1886). American Hill.

Obsessed with profession and ambition and not enough

low-brow back-sliding pleasure-taking pleasure. Longing for Golden Fridays and the complimentary car, an in-car phone, a pull-out couch. Eternal happy hours.

Grit-blown monoliths bounce measured hours of sunlight from their golden glass and stand for death, another Stonehenge in haphazard phalanx between Bow River and CPR tracks, (compressed) between two insoluble immovable configurations. Hanging there, in their moments of aspiration, the cranes wait for another boom to announce itself, another graveyard to rear headstones.

Quadrant Three : Denizen

Habitué, hooked, a citizen of. Within this enclosure (Calgary) the city a centre of spokes, empenned. (What does home mean?) Frequential, inhabiting. Spearpoints found in plowed fields east of the city (12 000 years old). Teepee rings, medicine wheels, effigies: Blackfoot, Sarcee, Stoney.

Boucher de Niverville: may have gone as far as Calgary, may have seen (1751) David Thompson and Peter Fidler. Then only the glacial valleys and the foreland thrust sheets (foothills) predicating the Rockies. Palliser. Come and gone. NWMP. Calgary no fur-trader's post but a mountie set-up (1875, F-troop). And Brisebois with no leg to stand on and only Brisebois Drive left (not even a trail) before Macleod and Hardisty. Desert nomads, transient denizens. Arriving and leaving, citizens of their own rules: Ex-mounties, Ex-speculators, Ex-Metis buffalo hunters, Ex-arrivals. Nomadic ranchers converging from the wide, cattle-sweeping country around.

Not so smart either: in 1890 everybody failed the territorial university entrance exam.

And the first police chief (couldn't compete with the NWMP) rigged dice games to pocket fines. Always boostermen, the ever proliferating real-estate outriders. And someone is waiting to write a story about Calgary quarrymen, a fastidious quarryman covered in sandstone dust as the lead in this romantic sound et lumière. Brothels to the east, up past Nose Creek. Some Germans and Italians, more Chinese: "the mongolians in our midst" (an unspecified citizen). Ango-Saxon, English-speaking, Protestant.

Nobody famous.

But angular and affronted frame houses jutting roofs into the acrid sky. And everywhere picket fences fencing out the prairie, fencing houses from themselves and each other, the neat divisions of denizens. Home of chinooks ("disarming winter of its severity"). Erotic in intent ("blizzards are unknown"). A lie, but there are always those who lie, continue to lie. Believe it, you say, blizzards are known and not only in the passive sense. The great snow of May, 1986, there were no tracks.

And yes, the denizens of this city, huddled in basement suites, climbing to apartments in the upper stories of large frame houses. Declarations: bumper stickers and license plates ("I'd rather push this car a mile than buy from PetroCan"); ("You're ugly and your mother dresses you funny"). You too. ZZZAP. MBA. The denizens of automobiles, grinding their teeth, whistling, moving their lips in sing-along drive up and down the trails, back and forth from quadrant to quadrant, moving, moving, the natives are restless, up over the coulees and down, west, west west west, to Banff and the mountains. (Where does home mean?)

Begun by the oldest occupation, the nomadic herding of grazing animals. Ranchers unsettled, the cattle themselves moving, always moving, their cattle kingdom a transported and elegiac shuffle. With the endless arrival of the CPR, a cadence established and ingrained. Restlessness, an historic restlessness, following the backs of beasts. Sleep on the ground, ride again in the morning. This companion of settlement. Here, this place.

And the Sarcee woman in the Co-op store turning over running shoes (related to Deerfoot), her hair knifing over her face. You edge past her, but always want to touch that encarved posture: she knows home better than you do, she knows where it is. And the lanky man slouched down on his backbone in the Plaza Theatre, sitting through the still ads for cultural artefacts, alone at the end of an aisle and still there the next week, the next month, endlessly watching moving movies of the world. And the denizen who cannot help (her) (him) self, cannot resist rushing under the swift silence of the LRT train, surprised by the impact, that it can be mute and still so solid. Between platforms all movement insubstantial, like the river below bridges lying still despite eroded banks. And some cowboy singers wailing against clinked glasses, trying to earn themselves another checkered shirt, and the best boots made anywhere in the world (this is the truth): boots.

"This is Ernest C. Manning and the Prophetic Bible

Institute's Back to the Bible Hour coming to you from Calgary, Alberta, in the foothills of the Canadian Rockies" (You Could Hear His Capitals). The horse on Eighth Avenue, paint flaking and chipped, a dead horse, a dry wind, a quiet hockey player.

You fail to believe that others can read the passion within you. You pretend not to see theirs. Who dares to confess to feeling, to anger, to rage, to joy. Not here. Stay calm, keep moving, don't look up. Above you hang the boomtown ghosts, half-finished buildings, struts and ceilings between gaping floors. The skeletons within your skins. You are those ghosts, con/ and de/struction, shareholders and mortgagees, full of sites and demolition.

Drink up.

Picturesquely situated so as to be within easy reach of the brewery, Calgary extends right and left, north and south, up and down, in and out, expanding as she goes, swelling in her pride, puffing in her might, blowing in her majesty and revolving in eccentric orbits around a couple of dozen large bars which close promptly at 11:30 right or wrong (Bob Edwards).

The York. The King Edward. The Alberta Hotel, the longest bar. Anywhere. Wait. Brewing and malting. Exporting dead meat. Quarrying sandstone. Right or wrong.

Transient: the nomadic legacy of the ranchers, east of the north/south route of prehistoric man, balloons drift overhead. Denizen: to live here you must move, although the stones command stillness, and the grass demands its own growing. Home is a movement, a quick tug at itself and it packs up. Call yourself a taxi and consult a map. A blur. And these discreet defections Calgary's denizens.

You do live here. Habitants of a glass sky and cardboard mountains shining offstage, checking Nose Hill for the moisture levels and never daring to kiss. You may dance Electric Avenue, eat on the Stephen Avenue Mall, grow cabbages in your back yard, rent out your basement, buy kitchen slicers and suitcases. Afraid to hang your masks on your walls, choose not to recognize moments of iconography: that you will probably stay here, die here, and perhaps even have yourself buried.

QUADRANT FOUR : OUTSKIRTS OF OUTSKIRTS

Calgary as quadrant, the sweep of a long-armed compass quartering the city NW/NE/SE/SW, segmented. Each quadrant leaks outward up the hills, along the coulees in a sprawl of roofs. But the REAL city south, inched it ways southward, money and business moving down from the low and gravelled Bow. No designations needed there, neither SW or SE until years later, it was the north that needed division and indication, North over the river, squatters and whores. The divisions/labyrinthine began. And when they talked "annex" NW kept at arm's length, safely out there.

Offered the streets names: Aaron/Jacob/Joshua (him again)/ Matthew/Mark/Luke/John/Esther/Sarah/Moses/Mark/Jeremiah; proper names of biblical intention, but subsumed (1912) by numbers, the sweet anonymity of 6th. Only Kensington left unnumbered and itself. An acrostic of place, 4th St. SE far away from 4th St. NW, divided into quarters and beyond the quarters suburbs themselves divided and subdivided.

. There has to be a minotaur somewhere. How to find yourself: see map. A majority of roads are named by number. Within the quadratic network 14th Ave. NW will run east-west in the northwest quadrant. Confusion.

Where is home? But from the outside, as early [wo]man a nomad wandering the prairie? From Nightingale east, moving west toward only a cleft in the hills, no evidence of city. And the pretence of buildings a slight inflection that swells as the body moves. The mountains overweigh all and when you dip south into the valley of the Bow the gaunt buildings appear, innocuous from this angle buried in themselves. And black, enigmatic. Unless you rise the right hillcrest at dawn, none of the golden flash that you have been led to expect.

From High River south, the old 2A leading itself north into appropriation, and the curve of double road that splits the huddled suburbicarian purlieus, outskirts of outskirts outskirted by those same foothills (are we in Lethbridge yet?), the overflung devouring edges stitching themselves into the ground. The ground, that yellow and black prairie ground between the fingers crumbling and soft. The foothills/foreland thrust sheets. And in your swing up through Millarville, Priddis, Bragg Creek and Morley the fortress begins to tower and sway, sown dragon's teeth that have grown themselves into monoliths without sacred sites at their bases, without pictographs and secret springs, and Uluru (that red nose in the Australian desert) complete in their unscalability.

Except for the window washers (of course). Except for the

falling accountants, except for the clefts and ledges of hurt that have all been smoothed down, polished over into a flat blank surface, refracting only itself. You too can jump.

And from the (far from Ellesmere) bush and parkland, Edberg, Bashaw, Tees, Lacombe (who taught you to forget Siksika), Olds and Didsbury and Carstairs a descent. That snaky arrival between the sexual clefts of the hills again surprised at the arrogance of those other coulees brooding on themselves in a pretence at centre, an underground that repels. Calgary is a place to run away from, although you claim to have run to it. And everyone pretends to be from somewhere else, not here, no babies born in this city except reluctantly, extracted from their mother's bodies in a storm of protest. Children born in moving vehicles: the C-train, buses, pickup trucks (inevitable gun racks), airplanes, moving vans.

An acrostic of place: if there were time to count muffler shops and Sleepeazy motels, faster and faster food and the secret motives of car dealerships (pricing themselves on windshields), you would never be found. Again. But there are labyrinths in the shopping malls, bubbles of light and air that claim closure, insist on wholeness and order, and you wandering, lost, cannot find the door you came in or any door at all and behind the shop window mannequins there is nothing: darkness, a bed, a small room full of stifled whispers that pretend to be obscene. Strip malls too: a dry cleaners, a Chinese restaurant, an uncrashed bank, pasting themselves onto the crossword puzzle of street.

You begin to look for lovers in these labyrinths of solar light. In the secret floors of hotel rooms, hotels interlocked by Plus 15s, ghostly vaginas: in one green room you bathe together, splash each other. In another you lie side by side, breathing gently. You are seldom locked together, coital, sex is too playful for Jericho and two pieces of the puzzle might connect. What would happen then – all the interlocking bridges (Louise and Langevin) (Louise, that princess, should be buried soon) unnecessary – all the trails (Crowchild, Marquis de Lorne, Shaganappi, Deerfoot) overruled, all 3 000 kilometres of paved road bypassed in a flyover of lust, for once, lust.

You need practice in the geography of lust. You need to find lovers in used bookstores, take someone else's clothes from the cleaners, invade the bushes of Spruce Cliff. There are incipient coitions between lonely watchers at the Plaza and playground bodies lying on their backs in the grass. Snow bodies. As far from Russia as carnal knowledge and its dyings.

Freeways stop abruptly, refuse to handle themselves into the hills farther than they are, abandonment in a fringe of crumbling asphalt. Plus 15s drop into space and connect nothing. Paths Russiantate a darkness of wooded coulee impossible to return from. Mud rooms front the marble foyers of postmodern buildings, log houses hewn into a visceral cry against glass. Who can find you here, a clumsy bawling beast in the centre of a web of thread, a cat's cradle of encapturement?

Located by confluence, the Bow and Elbow jointing them-selves an impassable lock. Without their deliberated quadrant you scramble in hollow streets and scanty hills, looking to the escarpment above, the sharp edge of Shaganappi coulee cutting off the mountains. In the squats and dry electricity of basement flats where printmakers select inks and artists draw faces (faces of women looking sidelong at one another), in the quarrels of the colleges and schools, students foundering into a sadly chosen ritual, there is still the labyrinth of stone.

The fossils of lost centuries embedded in walls, an architect's drawing of place. Brachiopods shine through their sealed surface, erypsids genuflect. You too are sheathed in prehistoric stone, the gravestones of Jericho before the walls tumble down.

Shout Calgary, this growing graveyard.

N

EXPLORATION SITE : ELLESMERE

N

ELLESMERE, woman as island

Anna Karenina should have escaped to Ellesmere.

If Tolstoy had suffered her, if she hadn't been a woman created and governed by a blind and obstinate man. This is a remedy you want to propose to her, Ellesmere, as if it were a nectar she could swallow or inhale. A consummate escape from Vronsky and Karenin, Ellesmere, that most northerly of extreme Arctic islands, probably un/named when Tolstoy invented her, probably unheard of, like Anna herself. A lost heroine. Lost in Russian, lost in love, lost in the nineteenth century. The especial lostness of an invented character whose inventor revenged himself on her through the failings he invented for her.

Anna. Her paginated presence makes you want to rescue her, offer her alternatives. Read her again, give her a second chance, another life, a different fiction.

You are at Ellesmere. You have escaped to Ellesmere. Her island, tabula rasa, awayness so thoroughly truant you have cut all connexion to all places far from Ellesmere. This is what you long for. Anna must have too.

Ellesmere is absence, a hesitation where you can pretend there are no telephones in the world, no newspapers, no banks, no books. You are only a body, here in this Arctic desert, this fecund island. Lungs, fingers, a stomach, legs and feet. This fragile world far tougher than you are, a floating polar desert for all characters to emulate.

Here you are closer to Russia than to yourself.

And why not dream of Siberia? It must be similar, although you have never been there, except in fiction. Siberia is an imaginary setting: you wait for it to suggest itself, for visits to be proposed. You would accept immediately, and there read only Canadian books.

But you are on Ellesmere.

You are camping, the two of you. You can list what you carry, what rides in your packs as you hike out from Lake Hazen, up the Abbé River toward Glacier Pass. A tent, big enough for two, but lightweight, its grey-brown skin between you/perpetual daylight. A sleeping bag each, two sleeping bags that can be zipped together for warmth or pleasure. A light camping burner, a Whisperlite. Three bottles of fuel. Two aluminum pans, two tin plates, two knives, two forks, two spoons. A spatula. *Anna Karenin*.

Just a minute. The spatula has nothing to do with *Anna Karenin* (except that it is lighter), although the plastic flask of Benedictine is connected. Your tripled socks and hiking boots are essential, spliced to ground. But the two heavy elastic ankle supports that you carry have nothing to do with *Anna Karenin*, nothing at all. You take them because you are worried about your ankle, the ligament you goddamn tore at Rudy Wiebe's lodge. You cannot afford to have the ankle give out on you now, although that was two years ago. You have: two pairs of long johns, two t-shirts, a heavy sweater, an Anorak, five pairs of socks, a pair of gloves, a toque. You have your toothbrush and some sunscreen. You have your contact lens solution.

You have *Anna Karenin*.

Easy to decide what to take on a camping trip, especially if you must carry everything you need to survive on your back: as little as possible.

You permit yourself the idea of one book.

This one book much more difficult than packing the clothes you do not take. One book for an entire eight days extreme deprivation. You can read one, two books a day. What if this single book is not enough? unsatisfactory? just plain bad?

You ransack bookstores, comb your shelves. You cannot take a hardcover, too heavy. Why do you reject a Canadian novel? Not so strange perhaps. Canadians without the slightest notion of Ellesmere, they look incredulous when you mention the name, ask, "Where's that?" Perhaps it is for poets to imagine Ellesmereland's space, its un/read isolation. Earle Birney the only contender. Sadly, you replace him on your shelf, poetry too sparse. You must find a novel, a thick, emphatic novel.

White nights.

You can read all night. The novel will have to be thicker than emphatic.

White nights did not ride south through Edberg and Edmonton, but between June and July the north glowed. The white nights you remember from Yellowknife held their own twilight, were not as undark as nights toward the pole. The sun rotates you, moving from the lake to the mountains and then back to the lake. You are never without it, although around six or seven it eases to shadow in this shadowless expanse.

And if you were a character in the implacable mote of a reader's eye, then would you live within white nights? Or dark pages? Which would be preferable, the cage of book, the open glare of sun?

An Anna?

You dare not trust the thick emporiums of popular books sold by the pound, airport books, cheats with vague characters and formula events. Now a conflict, now a sex scene. Bodice rippers. You have read one recently, despite yourself, furious at its sordid pawings of grammar. You finger the elegant bindings of the slender novels you re-read so often: Duras, Engel, Wolfe. No, they belong elsewhere, on other beaches, other islands. You scan heavy, proteinous writers, can do nothing except defect to Russia. Is it the waiting revolution? the nineteenth century? that echo of wolves and frozen wastes?

Dostoyevsky. Tolstoy: rampaging male egos with their gambling and renunciations.

"Take *War and Peace*," suggests Rudy Wiebe. He would, having once insisted that the reason women will never be GREAT writers is because they do not set themselves great subjects. "Like what?" you asked him then, furious, offended. "Like war and peace," he said in his Yahweh voice. "Women write only out of their viscera." The word *viscera* in his mouth scornful and repellent, plump with blood and bread. Since then you've learned the viscera of men larger and more dangerous, hidden as they are in an inflated sense of themselves centring the subject of greatness. War and peace exactly what you wish to leave behind in lower Canada. But you take *Anna Karenin*.

And why do you not carry a book written by a woman, one of your own reading your own? Why Anna, a self-indulgent character created by a man who couldn't imagine women enacting anything more interesting than adultery or mother-hood. Prescripted choices: mothers, saints or whores. Why Karenina, with Tolstoy at the pen, Tolstoy mad with theological tracts, with pleas for vegetarianism, with fulminations against liquor and tobacco? Tolstoy the sermonizer convinced that women were the seat of corruption, Tolstoy the moralist, Tolstoy the refusnik? A man so childish he ran away from home at the age of eighty-two, following his viscera?

The physical *Anna Karenin* that you read in Masterpieces of Russian Literature (in translation), for Peter Rolland (your Polish-American Russian professor), Penguin, an acceptable translation, a little dog-earred, on your shelf now for some fifteen years, since Edmonton. You read *Eugene Onegin* too and *The Diary of a Madman*, *The Nose*, *The Overcoat*, *A Hero of Our Time*, *Poor People*, *Notes from Underground*, *Crime and Punishment*, *Fathers and Sons*, *Childhood*, *The Cossacks*, *The Death of Ivan Ilyich*. A male course, now that you look at it, a very male course, and you must have gone too far, gotten carried away, *Anna Karenin* not on the list for Russian 320, you invented the necessity to read her yourself. Despite Tolstoy. Looking for an image of a woman, even one scripted by him.

What do you imagine, that you can dream Tolstoy a sister or a lover beyond his flawed imaginings, the characters that shape the body and brains of a woman more and less than his benighted

Anna? Islands neither preach nor convert, you will have to live with her.

On Ellesmere you want to forget the world's war and peace and read about love. Even love as doomed as you know Anna's to be.

So you take Tolstoy's eight hundred and fifty pages as a lesson, to solve a problem in how to think about love; to solve a problem in the (grave) differences between men's writing and women's writing; to solve a problem in sexual judgment. To investigate viscera and mirrors; passions and polemics. Even though you know you'll be stuck with Tolstoy, that the order and the rules are male, that he writes Anna no choices.

You are trying to learn indifference, practice scientific curiosity.

You want to read yourself (in a mirror) and Anna a fictional mirror of a male reading of women. Perhaps you can un/read her, set her free. There on that desert island, between the harebells and the blue dreaming of glaciers.

You know no Annas, no women named Anna. Some Annes, some other Anns. But no Anna (except that Anna, clearly mad, unravelled by grief, your Edmonton landlady's sister-in-law slave whose weeping you heard through the wall, and who had no train to fling herself under). You know at least a hundred Annas, stranded in fictional love affairs written by men who do not know that Ellesmere exists. Come to that, women are all Annas, caught or not, Annas sweating their way from one day to the next. They know the wars within their orbits, between children and husbands and lovers, need and desire and the desperate necessities of symmetry, how they will be always and forever culpable, exiled for their visceras, eviscerated for their exiles.

Anna Karenina should have gone to Ellesmere.

The heart can live through a desert island, a Siberia. And also Ellesmere.

Where you must read her over, through the transparency of Tolstoy's blame, his punitory withholding of erotic and emotional ease. Anna, poor Anna, dead before she begins, the end already read. You know where she is going, have pre/read that destination. But re/reading her, in Ellesmere a/new, reading her whole, you can re/write her too. The un/read face of desolation, Anna in Ellesmere's brief summering.

Oh Anna.

Getting to Ellesmere easier than it should be. Bob prepares for weeks, over-prepares, you think, but he has more experience than you, has a better idea of what you need. You are up early, catch the taxi to the airport, a clear-eyed, clear-headed day with the Calgary sky a sizzling arc. Everything on schedule, your packs arriving in Edmonton even before you do – perhaps you have already taken this trip and are only following your future. Perhaps your record of reading *Anna Karenin* on Ellesmere is already written, already un/read. But you have never been so close to falling under a version of train, that grubby dayliner from Edberg suddenly enormous, bearing down on history and fiction.

And what do you know about Russia? St. Vladimir, Vales, Stribog, Khors, Dazhbog, the battle at the River Kalka, Ivan Kalitp, Ivan IV (the terrible), the Zealots of Piety, the Raskol (created Doukhobors), despite Peter the Great, the eight gubyernyiya: Kiev, Moscow, Smolinsk, Archangel, Kazan, Azov, Siberia, St. Petersburg; salt, alcohol and tobacco, but baroque and then Catherine the Great who deposes another Peter (III?) and Paul I tries to fix up his mother's mess, but gets murdered anyway, and Alexander I dies of typhoid, and the unforgettable Napoleonic war of 1812, and all those Edmonton references to the czar, even Pushkin who presumably perfects Russian as a literary language. All the names have changed now. How to read through, past this male historiographical fiction? We all come out of Gogol's *Overcoat* ? Do we?

Nothing, you know nothing about Russia.

And even less of Ellesmere. It is there. It has always been there.

The Yellowknife/Resolute plane full of arctic adventurers and outfitters, strange southerners seeking something stranger. Tour groups, hiking and kayaking groups. The flight north speaks its own grammar of stone and tree, water and sky. Time falls under a train. The plane drones. You sleep, doze, ache oddly. Before the long dip into the Arctic Ocean, Resolute Bay afloat with ice but the ocean green, open. Lancaster Sound and Barrow Strait leading clear into the un/found Northwest Passage. Cornwallis Island.

Resolute barks, its babies cry, the bingo machine in the hall rattles. The village still, as if snow needs to come, as if waiting for its winter when dogs and snowmobiles can roar to life. Furs cast over railings, sleeping bags wilt on the stony ground. Stones, here are stones. This village, trying to hold its own against the airport, odds enormous and re/settled. The airport presuming only women and carvings. The road between the airport and the village long and dusty, an occasional yellow poppy bent against the wind.

Anna. All Annas women written by men, now re/read by women. The reader un/reading the Anna.

Vengeance is mine, and I will repay.

She is supposed to represent the epitome of the nineteenth century psychological novel, its high-water mark. High water, Anna, think of that. Is high water the Arctic Ocean? Past the high arctic: the middle north, the far north, the extreme north. You can read her only at extreme north.

Go north, Anna, go north. If there are westerns, why can there not be northerns? Northerns of the heart, harlequins in reverse, bodice rippers of paled faces and quick glances, able to withstand the scrutiny of relentless light or relentless dark. Anna has been punished too long. Take her with you to Ellesmere. You're sure she's never been there, no one else is likely to have carried a woman as difficult, as lengthy, as goddamned heavy as she is along.

You are fogged in. White rags hang from the chunky ice off/shore. Nothing to do but wait, a northern patience. Read the *New Yorker*. In a place where no one cares about New York, where New York does not exist, where the rest of the world is illusion, only a place to read about. American missionaries here to teach Sunday school – Christian Bible school? – to the Inuit children. You are unforgivably profane in light of what you read as pure stupidity, but their faces register blindness, a bland compliance with their calling. The Inuit children of Resolute need American Christian fundamentalist missionaries? Jesus and Anna Karenina save them.

You are saving Anna until you get to Ellesmere. You read about cane cutters in Florida, their strange dance with sugar and heat, snakes in the fields.

Packed, ready to go, waiting for the fog to lift. A five-hour flight from Resolute, midnight before you reach Lake Hazen, then the tent to pitch. If you get in. The ceiling low, heavy cloud cover, you may have to turn back or stay in Eureka. There is no need for leave-taking, no formal goodbye, only the step up into the twin otter, and the tight seat, the metal seatbelt. You wear: long underwear, heavy pants, a t-shirt, another shirt, a sweater, an Anorak. You look inelegant, but warm. You feel wonderful. Clearing the runway, the toy bay of Resolute recedes below.

("Christ," says the pilot, while you wait in the Bradley shack. "He was sweating razor blades. Coming up the lake wasn't sure he could get the plane off.")

Discovery. What to call the first moment a place lodges in your memory, what to call the first moment place emplaces itself in naming. Edberg was always there, an initial seeing that you don't remember, small as you would have been, two. Edmonton, that city as initial, forever a jagged mouth of buildings rearing past the refineries from the east, a patchy development after the high yawn of the Beverly Bridge. And Calgary, the first time you saw Calgary you were ten? Twelve? You cannot remember its announcement, only prescient presence, and the mountains past it, the way you read it now, as a well-groomed cemetery.

Ellesmere will appear like a languid body below you, the island only waiting finally to float into a geografictione, like Anna waiting so long backstage on the yet-to-arrive, the interminably delayed train. No trains on Ellesmere. Stubborn muskox and inevitable glaciers. And other inevitabilities, mountains and rivers and the brief exquisite summer just three weeks long, never much above ten degrees, snow only gone long enough to come back again.

Do trains exist to remind us of futility? Of the always coming and going, meeting and farewelling that love affairs demand? Now you see them in airports, those lingering, frantically compressed caresses, but in the nineteenth century they would have been on the platforms of train stations (still are, in Europe, you've seen them), with the steam from the locomotive huffing around the bottoms of skirts, and the noise of the porters and their carts a background motivation. They were footless, then, on those platforms, as if walking on cloud, and the soot, the absolute soot would have been inescapable, a fine black dust over everything. And before you even open the book you know that Tolstoy bought it in a railway station, with everyone feuding over him, he his own Anna living out his own novelistic fantasy of the perfect death it was necessary to run toward. You must live up to your fictions, all there is to it; you must help yourself achieve geografictiones of the soul, moments of erasure only available in fiction and on desert islands.

You worry that your boots will give you blisters.

Cornwallis drones past quickly, flight too far east to see Little Cornwallis. The ocean here, Wellington Channel, one huge jigsaw, the ice pieces laid out on a giant board waiting for winter

to put them together again. Puzzle-ice. Mesmerizing, its slow
wash and float, its conundrum melting and reappearance. The
chunks themselves islands and the arctic ocean between a liquid
light. (You've dreamed of it, this puzzle-ice has floated through
your dreams, and you were riding one of the chunks, feet planted
wide apart, floating on frozen water over water, the cold, cold
Arctic past Lancaster Sound and down into Baffin Bay.) But now
above the northern point of Devon Island, Grinnell Peninsula
and Arthur Fjord, Devon on the map shaped like a seal sticking
its head out of water, and then over the huge gap of Norwegian
Bay.

These names, every mapped configuration male/lineated. Is
this the answer to Tolstoy's question, "What then, can we do?"
Name, name, leave names on everything, on every physical
abutment, leave behind one's father's name, the names of other
men, the names of absent and abstracted/ideal women. Anna, has
she an island or a bay, an inlet? Is there an Anna Karenina Cape
in Russia? Don't ask how many Tolstoy inlets there must be.

Axel Heiberg Island. Who was he? Some Norwegian consul
who probably never even saw it, relied on (his friend?
acquaintance? emissary?) Otto Sverdrup to immortalize him, in
1899. He must be dead: yes, both of them, Sverdrup and
Heiberg. But the island is alive. Mountains, dazzled valleys, sheer
cliffs between spectacular fjords, drawn glaciers that edge down
centuries, inching immaculate blue over a ragged tear of coast.
The fjords plunge to surrender. Where the snow has melted the
land is red, crimson, madder rose, a brilliant brown, a
dazzlement. Rise and rise, over the Princess Margaret Range,
climbing to avoid the clouds, the roiling weather. Higher, higher,

bad weather ahead, above acceptable oxygen levels, the pressure zone. You take short deep breaths, difficult to breathe at all. Anna before she plunges between the wheels of the train cars, quick deep breaths, but she horrified at her unstoppable action, you elated. Higher, you want to shout to the pilot over the airplane's grind. Higher. But he is past the system and guiding the plane down again, Mokka Fjord and then Eureka Sound, the thin strip of it between Axel Heiberg and Ellesmere.

Eureka, the garden spot of Canada. It is raining, a cold, driving sleet on the gumbo airstrip. You slide out, slip footslapstick to the Bradley shack, wait, bad weather ahead, no guarantee the plane will get into Hazen. Might have to sleep here, wait it out, Eureka a sad movie set of shacks and corrugated iron, lost weather station unable to predicate either weather or future, Earle Birney's men who "guard the floes that reach to the Pole," who "watch the sky watch them." The science of the south dislocated across the sound from the silver mountains of Axel Heiberg.

But you are on Ellesmere, this mystery of polar desert, remote of all Canada's island flock. As far as it is possible to get away: and you will fly still farther north, not even close to Hazen yet, its eurhythmic allure.

In the Bradley shack you find a daily log kept by a lonely employee, his day-to-day chores a sad and homesick snowy spring, blizzards and broken generator, his writing down of every moment's movement in order to get through a few more days, a few more days before time swallowed him. The pilot swills Listerine (does it keep him awake?). You itch to open *Anna Karenin*, riding in the pocket of your jacket, but force yourself to wait, wait, necessary waiting. The plane waits for the radio, an impatient hour, then suddenly you are windmillrunning through the mud, the sky has lifted into high cloud, a pleasant – no, not evening – one o'clock in the morning.

White nights. Flying/flying past/through/into white nights over blue pack ice broken and rotten to brown, over icebergs floating belly/up and serene, over the incisement of glaciers and fjords. The land that never melts. And never melts. A frozen heart. It is July 27, snow cover like streaked cream.

Over Ellesmere, up Greely Fjord and Tanquery Fjord and the mountains swathed in ice two thousand meters thick, as old as the last ice age one hundred thousand years ago. Here is the place to read about love, to take readings on love, on passion: this thinly naked, perpetually frozen world.

And then Hazen plateau and Lake Hazen, the ice in the lake blotted with darker moments, past Henrietta Nesmith (who the hell was she? somebody's mother) Glacier and its mouth melting into Henrietta River and then Ptarmigan Creek and Blister Creek (your boots are starting to settle in), down, down in bright sunlight here in the middle of the night past the hump of McGill Mountain and the few scattered tents, the ragged drift of a Canadian flag and Hazen camp (abandoned), down, Johns Island (who the hell was he?) a thin pencil in the lake, down to a short bumpy landing on the old strip by the shore.

The plane unloaded, you put up your tent, Bezal makes coffee. It is bright sunlight, three o'clock in the morning. You fall into solid and clarified sleep.

But you have opened *Anna Karenin*. You have begun to read.

Inside your purple sleeping bag on your thermarest on the rocky shore of Lake Hazen, with your head pillowed on your extra sweater, you have begun to read this discontented text, this corpulent Russian novel that pretended for so long to read the essential psyche of the passionate woman succumbing to extreme and impossible passions, infecting all around her. Anna tried, convicted, condemned. You are on Ellesmere Island. You are in Russia. You are free to un/read yourself, home, Anna, the rest of Canada, all possible text.

Do you read that Lake Hazen is the largest lake in the polar regions, the largest lake north of the Arctic Circle? Do you read that Hazen Plateau is a peculiar kind of thermal oasis that succeeds in achieving relative warmth in the summer? Do you read that Ellesmere is a true polar desert, with only three centimetres of precipitation per year? Or do you dream these physical facts, these delicious imprimaturs?

Beginnings gather those dilatory moments when you hesitate, evaluate. Beginnings are when you need to locate where you are, with people or places. Introductions, mappings, initiations. Novels and life open cautiously.

Anna's brother an initiatory gesture, Prince Oblonsky and his indiscretion with the governess, the liberties he has taken newly discovered by his unhappy, deceived wife. Stiva is a likeable fellow all right, but a slut, sluttish with money, with food, with sex. The wrong epithet, you say, it should be profligate, only women are sluts. Time to un/read the language: Stiva is a slut. He is intended to act as brotherly prologue for Anna, you know that, his bad behaviour supposed to make you aware that it runs in the family, this amorality, this appetite. He a preemptive mirror for Anna, who is coming, coming, coming, on the yet-to-arrive and so-long-awaited train. Like Anna, a fashion-plate in appearance and opinion; like Anna, faced with innumerable impossibilities – *that it was impossible to put right or patch up their relationship because it was impossible to make her [his wife] attractive and lovable again or to turn himself into an old man incapable of love.* Stiva suffers from a mid-life (rather early) crisis, male menopause, perpetual unfaithfulness. Like Anna, his physical appearance, his sprightliness, bring a smile of pleasure to everyone's lips, this incorrigible womanizer, moving from governesses to ballet dancers to other women of the demi-monde, an inveterate debtor, a gourmandizing glutton. But *he* doesn't throw himself under a train, far from it. Tolstoy lets him get away with it. His eager curiosity about the first train accident: he loves all that is visibly affective, but forgets quickly, even after his sister's death giving dinners and talking as vivaciously as ever. Someone should push *him* under a train, his long-suffering wife might enjoy that pleasure.

Stiva convinces you that adultery is the conclusion of monogamy; organized sexuality is like organized crime: extortionist. Why him and not his sister?

Still, at the beginning you tolerate him because you know he is the reading route to Anna, he will bring her into the novel. And he does, he writes to Anna and implores her to come as intercessor to his distressed marriage, and she agrees, wires that she will come on the tomorrow of the novel's opening. Stiva an excuse for arrival, as much as an example of the familial tendency to succumb to disproportionate appetite. If you read Anna through her brother, you must mis/read her. For Stiva, although he can be momentarily discomfitted, is incapable of torment, and Anna, you know, is capable of (terrible) torment. Stiva is only the beginning of Tolstoy's double entendre, his dealing from the bottom of the deck.

Warming, the puzzle-ice in the lake begins to melt itself into open patches, push itself around. Somewhere in your hearing sleep the ice crawls onto shore, a dying chime, the high clear music of nature. Summer on Ellesmere. Thaw, a pure reading.

And Stiva procurer, pander to the reader, a tool for Tolstoy. He drags first Anna into the novel, then Vronsky, deliberately suggesting him to Levin as rival suitor for Kitty's hand. Indeed, Tolstoy uses (unreliable) Stiva to answer Levin's fore/shadowing question: *'Who is this Vronsky?'* Stiva offers an initial reading of Vronsky, but if you read Vronsky through Stiva, you must mis/read him.

> *'He is one of Count Kiril Ivanovich Vronsky's sons, and a fine sample of the gilded youth of Petersburg…Awfully rich, handsome, influential connexions, an aide-de-camp to the Emperor and a capital fellow into the bargain. But he is more than just a good fellow. From what I have seen of him here, he is cultured and very intelligent – a man who will go far.'*

Yes, a man who will go far, too far in seductions and travellings. Stiva procures your interest in Vronsky as much as later he is spectacularly unsuccessful in procuring Anna's divorce from Karenin. His persuasions are uneven. But you can count on him to pimp for you, to appear with a new character, a different diversion, to give an excellent dinner or to remind you of whatever else is comme il faut at a particular fictional moment. Stiva should make the casual reader uncomfortable, Stiva should make the plot-driven reader nervous. Stiva plotted from one fashionable moment to the next, determinedly temporal and motive-driven, willing always to sluff off responsibility and to move on to the next page, the next entertainment.

Ellesmere does not permit such readings, such bare-faced superficiality. Before you set out from Hazen camp you check your supplies, re-pack your pack. The day overcast, low cloud, a thin but penetratingly clear light. You want to put as much space between yourselves and the camp as you can manage, even the few (only five or six) tents there too much, too many people, smells and voices of humans grating and unbearable. You hike for three hours, stop by a stream to look at your map, decide where to go. This first day out not far, a few hours to get solidly away from any connexion with people or airplanes. Whenever you stop you settle yourself on a rock or a tussock of moss and pull Anna from your pocket. You are well past the beginning now, and waiting to read their meeting – Anna and Vronsky: con/cussion.

Vronsky steps onto the page first. He appears, coming in behind a lady at the Shcherbatsky home, and at this meeting Levin your pander, asking virtually the same question he asked Stiva earlier. *'But what kind of man was he?'* You read him through Levin's envious eyes: good-natured, handsome, freshly shaven, elegant. He is affable, excellently equipped for the treacherous ground of drawing room conversation, a kind of military tactical diversion where one treads topical land mines. The conversation he and Levin have about the country reads him best. He asks if it is not dull for Levin to live in the country, and when Levin rather churlishly insists that one is not dull in one's own company, Vronsky admits that he has never tried the country for long, but:

'I never felt so homesick for the country – Russian country, with bast shoes and peasants – as I did when I was spending a winter with my mother in Nice.'

Vronsky's homesickness when enjoying the pleasures of one of Europe's most fashionable watering holes reads him an entire novel before his final toothached departure to fight the Turks in Serbia. Despite his fashionable chameleonism, his ability to change his stripes in every situation, he is a product of Russia, and outside Russia he will perish. A determined dilettante capable of interesting himself in table-turning, peculiarly tenacious, steadfast. And Tolstoy makes Anna mis/read both his dilettantism and his steadfastness.

Anna's train arrives a few pages after Vronsky's. And now it is he who panders to the reader, first reads her for you; his reading establishing your novelistic embarkation of her. Her elegance and friendliness match his, but what makes him tarry is her vitality:

It was as though her nature were so brimming over with something that against her will it expressed itself now in a radiant look, now in a smile. She deliberately shrouded the light in her eyes but in spite of herself it gleamed in the faintly perceptible smile.

Anna is alive, she has stepped off the train from Petersburg directly into Vronsky's gaze, into his reading, and into yours. She insists on being read, eyes follow her wherever she goes. But she is not transparent. Her first words, again read for you through Vronsky, are words of friendly disagreement with a male voice, disembodied. *'All the same I do not agree with you'*, she says, and when the man replies that that is the Petersburg way of seeing things, she replies, *'Not at all, simply a woman's way.'* Already

Anna begs to differ, already she distinguishes her way of thinking from that of men. She dares to read differently, to read as woman. Vronsky, who listens intently to this exchange, does not read Anna's words well, although he reads her body very well indeed. You know this double reading will continue: Vronsky is always capable of reading Anna's body; it is her language, her text, he has difficulty with.

On Ellesmere, reading a consecrated pleasure. In Calgary, when you were packing, you reminded Bob to take a flashlight. "What for?" he asked, grinning. "In case I want to read at night," you said crossly. You always do this – wake up in the middle of the night and read, it is your engagement with yourself when you cannot dream. "You can," he said. "All night. Read without a flashlight. There's twenty-four hours of sunlight."

White nights, you had forgotten. And now you inhabit those white nights, their bending of the day into a different figuration, a time without dark, beyond dark; only in the evening a peculiar shading of the ground that reverses by the early morning so that the sun through the brown weave is hot, steady, at three AM intense with purpose. You wake up then, to the heat, look at your watch. *Anna Karenin* lies by your head. The book opens to your hand, your open eyes.

One thing about Anna: she is not the expected feminine principle, not a slim, streamlined adolescent, but a woman on the verge of flesh, with a full figure, solid. She cannot be a sapling because of her moral corruption; only adolescents are permitted to be virginal. Her flesh has appetite. And Ellesmere is a fat island, the tenth largest in the world, fat with the flesh of heated snow, of dazzling cold. Fat with distance, with unreachability, with mystery. Hard to configure as an island at first, sighted by William Baffin (how: from the shore/with a telescope/from his ship?) in 1616, but not explored until the nineteenth century. The nineteenth century island: the nineteenth century novel. But John Ross discovered parts of the coastline in 1818 (too much symmetry), and in 1852 the island was named, during the Inglefield expedition, for the Earl of Ellesmere. Why? Had he given them money? What did they read on those ice-bound shores that suggested the island should be named for him? And was their reading correct? Is it an Ellesmere, or something else, some other name that other beings spoke? There must be another name, somewhere, if one only had the eyes to read it.

Sir George Nares led an expedition of the Royal Navy (extensive exploration) in 1875 and 1876. Anna Karenina was being written; Tolstoy was having a fine time of it, writing what he called his first novel, the novel begun on March 18, 1873, out of seeing, three years earlier, the body of an undressed and dissected young woman who threw herself under a train from heartbreak over a love affair, although even earlier than that Tolstoy had expressed interest in writing a story about a "guilty" woman who should be pitied rather than despised. Already contradictions proliferate, in dates and motives, in readings.

Anna was published/punished by installment and, it seems, read the same way; in 1876 Tolstoy complains of being sick and tired of Anna, fed-up. He insists on a moral conclusion and a discussion of the validity of war in his epilogue; the editor, who was in favour of the Turkish war, refused to publish it, instead printing only a brief paragraph stating that since Anna was dead, the novel was over.

Tolstoy had to bring out his own epilogue. Serves him right.

Meanwhile, Ellesmere was being explored by Nares and his men, especially the naturalist H.W. Fielden, who collected rocks and fossils from the region between Lady Franklin (not again – there should be a veto on Franklin and all his relatives, all his unfortunate crew) Bay and Fielden Peninsula. Explored, not discovered. Forty-two hundred years ago hunting bands roamed beside the inlets and fjords of Hazen Plateau. They had a name for Ellesmere, you are sure of that.

Instead of finishing her off with platitudes and morals, Tolstoy should have let her run away, the way that you did, freed her to go to Ellesmere. You wonder if the news of Ellesmere reached Russia, if they heard about the newly noticed presence of another northern island, or if Siberia was enough, too much for them to bear.

They might have talked of it in those drawing rooms, perhaps Princess Tverskoy's where Anna sees Vronsky so frequently, although the saucy gossip required there would probably have yawned at the very thought of an English expedition exploring frigid wasteland unpopulated by any fashionable society and bereft of both theatre and scandal. An expedition excited over rocks and fossils (if they were visible from beneath the eleven-month snow cover), instead of balls and affairs, races and positions. Perhaps the Russians were sending out their own explorers, imploring them to come back with frozen islands/desolate distances. Wars and expeditions: the nineteenth century gapes with them.

And Anna, now that she has met Vronsky, how does she fare? Is the expedition she is about to set out on with him fated?

Tolstoy setting her up and then daring to be disappointed in her? Not Vronsky, of course, he doesn't bear the weight of moral umbrage. He has other interests. He is to be admired for his pursuit of Anna precisely because she is married and inaccessible; only a man who who pursues a young girl or a single woman is ridiculous. What is to be made of this falling in love, this instant affliction that enters at the eyes? They meet on the train, they appraise each other, they part cordially. They meet at the ball, they dance together, Anna leaves Moscow the next day. They meet again on a railway platform on the way back to Petersburg, they meet and meet and meet and meet until they succumb. Or Anna succumbs to him? Or they both succumb to Tolstoy's *shame, rapture, and horror,* his murderous analogy of murder. They might have succumbed to Ellesmere.

That is easy. After the first day, you are seduced. You have learned to watch your feet on the tussocky moss; your pack cleaves to your back. You ford the Snow Goose River, its swift delta icy and treacherous. Scouting for a narrow shallow place to cross, Bob tests different channels through the rocky bed. The water is numbing, direct melt from the glaciers above, and you are terrified of being pulled under. But Bob carries the packs across and then comes back for you. You prepare your feet as if you were a water-wading dancer, diver's socks inside your old runners. Take off your jeans and wear only your rain pants, tie them tightly around your legs. Waterproof, they hold back some of the freezing shock. You edge your way, the round stones rolling themselves smooth at the bottom of the river shifting under your weight, the water's fierce strength pushing/pulling, you stagger hand in hand through a river only up to your thighs, but treacherous and snarling as liquid tiger.

For a moment, transfixed in the swirling middle, you want to sink to your knees, submerge in this passionately shaped water pouring itself down from the perpetual glaciers of the Arctic. This river, the Snow Goose, would be an ideal death, better than the instant violence of trains, Anna, you would let go so peace-fully into a gradual numbing, numbing, numbing, the body nothing more than a stone rubbed smooth and tumbled over and over until the river mouth empties itself into Lake Hazen.

On the other side, you are triumphant, ecstatic, the afterglow of the water's engulfment like the wash of an orgasm. You have left everything behind now, all other humans, in crossing isolated yourself from even a suggestion of people. You stop, rest, dry out your runners and your magic socks. Amazing, these diver's socks: using the body's heat to warm the freezing water, the trapped water transfigured, as warm as skin itself.

Beside the river you read a few more snatches of Anna getting herself deeper and deeper into trouble or love, falling through an icy declension of desire. She will get hypothermia from this desperate expedition of the heart; it is worse than glacier melt.

That is the kind of thing that Princess Myagky would say, bare-faced, bare-boned. She a brilliant shard of glass in the middle of those mannered and stifling drawing rooms. You do not remember her from your earlier reading, enthralled to discover her now, the naïve and rough *Enfant terrible*, so good at cutting short incestuously spiteful conversations. Saved by her appearance, *a stout, red-faced, fair-haired lady who wore an old silk dress and had no eyebrows or chignon.* It is the missing eyebrows and absent chignon that you particularly relish, her refusing extra hair, not caring who reads her pluckedness.

She makes you speculate on hirsuteness in fashionable expectation. Women are admired for having hair – on their heads, but admonished to scrape it from our legs, our underarms, our crotches. Shaping the self to a bland dis/surface, no tendrils to distract from contour, a de-sexualizing. Anna's tendrils, more than anything else, get her into trouble. They imply sexuality, that she too can escape from decorous containment. Her *wilful curls* are always escaping *at her temples and on the nape of her neck.* There it is: she's trouble. Tendrils: tendre: tender: tendre: to stretch, that botanical filamentous organ that permits a plant to climb, climb toward the light. She cannot be contained. Damn Tolstoy, forcing on her physical manifestations of her struggle against constraint.

But the Princess Myagky, who has a moustache but no eyebrows, is a different story, a practitioner of nakedness: naked admissions, naked observations, naked facts.

> 'They asked my husband and me to dine, and I was told that the sauce alone cost a thousand roubles,' said the Princess Myagky loudly, conscious that everybody was listening. 'And a very nasty sauce it was, too: some green mess. We had to invite them back, and I made a sauce for eighty-five kopecks and everyone was quite satisfied. I can't afford thousand-rouble sauces.'

Nor can you. The food that you carry is mostly dried, with some fruit, some chocolate. The Princess Myagky watches over the dinner you cook on your single burner, some kind of pasta with a nasty green sauce impossible to eat. She is reading your sauce while you are reading hers, the first person in the novel to speak her mind straight-forwardly (except for gloomy Levin, whose sections you skip over).

The Princess Myagky is too much fun, you know she will not be permitted to continue for that very reason; Tolstoy will shut her out of the novel, ignore her salty presence. So you relish her, with her green sauce (asparagus? spinach? pea?) and her roubles and her down-to-earthiness, only present in this drawing room because she is a princess, and because she is mis/read.

> *The effect produced by anything the Princess Myagky said was always the same, the secret of that effect being that, though she was often, as now, beside the point, what she said was simple and contained sense. In the society in which she lived such plain-speaking passed for the greatest wit. The Princess Myagky could never understand why this was so, but she knew that it was, and took advantage of it.*

The Princess reads with devastating accuracy, but although she is mis/read, she reads her mis/reading with the most astute of readings. You trust her opinion not only on pukey green sauce, but on love and marriage and on Anna's husband, Karenin.

When the conversation partakes of love, nibbles at sowing wild oats and *mariages de convenance*, the Princess says thoughtfully, '*In my young days I was in love with a deacon…I don't know that it did me any good.*' Deacons never do, Princess; they incite a gloomy prurience that does no one good, despite love. In your young days, you were in love with a deacon too: thank god you didn't marry him, saved yourself that trouble; although you've hit a few deacons and their daughters along the way. Believe it, there's nothing worse, they concoct their own unsavory sauces.

And the Princess places your notion of expert and important and to-be-respected and hallowed and cooked-for and cleaned-up-after and sighed-for and long-suffered and god knows determinedly-hung-onto husbands in clear perspective. You could prescribe her to a few wives you know. Not that it would help their afflictions.

> *'If our husbands were not so fond of talking, we should see things as they are; and it's my opinion that Karenin is simply a fool. I say it in a whisper...but does not that explain everything? Before, when I was told to consider him clever, I kept looking for his ability and thought I must be too stupid myself to see his cleverness; but directly I said to myself, he's a fool — only in a whisper, of course — it all became quite clear.'*

Ah, Princess, what you whisper to yourself; if only Tolstoy listened to you more.

When the Princess appears on Ellesmere, wonderfully hairless and yet with a lovely glossy moustache above her long lip, she sits perched on a rock, and invites you to abjure society: they are always talking about some fright, they are always assassinating one character or another. The same everywhere you tell her, she doesn't need to blame Russian society and the nineteenth century for that. Isn't that why you had a revolution? you ask her. Oh, I wouldn't know a thing about it, she insists. We were all supposed to have been more or less killed in it, but I wouldn't know a thing about it. Still, she says thoughtfully, pulling at the fingers of her green gloves, we probably deserved it. We had such awful husbands. Tolstoy, are you listening?

The Princess' opinion of Karenin is exactly your impression of Levin, whom you want to avoid, will a/void. He is not here on Ellesmere, although he is in the book. You will not let him out, you cannot stand his fulminating, his pseudo-philosophizing. When you get to him, you snap the book shut, wrap a thick elastic band around it, beginning to suffer from its exposure to campfires and mosquitoes, rock dust and river water. He would never understand Ellesmere, or why you are here. He would insist on talking about productivity and the nature of work, he would question why there are no trees in this exquisite desert. Tolstoy feeds you Levin as exemplary sludge. Even his doubt-fulness, his grappling with meaning and suicide is exemplary. Nothing makes him happy, except perhaps losing himself in physical work. As alternate to Anna, Levin makes you furious. Marriage for him may be a series of well-kept secrets, but he would still condemn you to its grasp, its stifling domesticity, its limiting goal of motherhood. You can almost hear his gloomy repetition of Saint Paul's "it is better to marry than to burn."

Campfires. No, there are no trees here, nothing but the springy moss on the tussocks that you walk, that you stumble past. Strange, these clumps of permafrost, roundheaded under the ground, irregular. It is as if you step over thinly buried heads, tufted and waiting in a permafrost sleep. You are learning sure-footedness all over again; one mis/step will result in a twisted ankle and you pinned on the landscape until the other can hike the long miles back to camp, where the radio isn't working anyway, and you'd have to wait for the next plane a week from now. It is comforting to you that no one can rescue you, that you can't be saved by someone's good intentions. You are developing a dazzling dislike for the good intentions of the novel, the way they insinuate themselves into a perfectly miserable life and try to cure it, the way they maneuver your reading.

Levin (a.k.a. Tolstoy) reads Anna in the same way he mis/reads the outward appearance of all women. He tells Oblonsky, '*all fallen women are the same*', he separates them into the finite categories of fallen and unfallen. Are islands all the same? Is Ellesmere the same as Baffin, as Vancouver, as the Kerguelens? Only, obviously, if they are happy: *all happy families are alike but an unhappy family is unhappy after its own fashion.*

And Ellesmere is a happy island, happy in its strange remoteness, its inaccessibility. Unaltered much by [ ]man, simply habitation for the hares hopping idly through the brief meadows, the muskoxen you come upon at the back of Omingmak Mountain. Over a small rise, you find them lowering, snorting for you to keep your distance: short-chested beasts with massive heads and humps. More hair than brains, they are shaggy and itchy, their fur falling in patches.

So if there are no trees, where do you burn campfires? In fiction anything is possible. But Ellesmere is no fiction and it has no trees, that clean-swept northern desert of desire. At night (white night), you discover that you can have a fire, if you gather together the dead roots of the low tundra willow – hardly even a tree but a plant that clings to the ground – and crumble them, enjoy a brief, flaring blaze, a short, sharp celebration of your light-lengthened day. The thin stems that you scrape together, twigs, scanty fingers that crawl along the ground in search of moisture. Some, green and pliable, are clearly finding enough to stretch themselves, slowly, intricately, over the frost-heaved gravel. Others, grey branchlets, brittle and ash-dead. You gather handfuls of these, pile them together in a careful miniature pyramid and cup your hands around a match to incite flame. Crouched, you inhale its brief smoke, trade the plastic thermos cup of Benedictine back and forth. A few sips for the end of the hiking day, a few drops scattered as libation on the tundra.

Cushion plant tundra this must be called, these plants visible only when you drop to your knees. From standing height, it seems as if you walk across a ground cover of desolation, shards of rock, sand, the occasional clump of purple sagafrass, a sudden yellow dotting of Arctic poppies.

And Anna, there you see her, herself in brilliant yellow, standing tall beside – always – an unidentified man dressed in a black frock coat. This is presumably an image you have gotten from the movies, although you have never seen the famous movie with – nor do you want to – the famous actress playing Anna. Which man is it, the one in the black clawhammer coat, Karenin or Vronsky? Perhaps Oblonsky, her brother, or even Levin, standing severely a correct three feet away, afraid she will contaminate him. Or Tolstoy, still blaming Anna for what she's done, he's made her do. She floats serenely over the tundra, her tiny feet poised, her hands together. The yellow poppies bend as she passes. The back of the man in the black frock coat is always sternly turned away, his shoulders severe, his hands clenched and rigid. He has none of her calmness, her presence: her bearing is joyful, his posture denies her.

The yellow Arctic poppies so much less proper than the wifely blue harebells. Their slender, hairy stems bend to the ink inside their yellow cups, bright against the grey-green ground. Small wells of ink inside their stems, their cups, as if they are flowers of writing, writing themselves strewn over Ellesmere. Their tiny burstings an opening shout, again and again. Elegant in the wind, blown and torn, ragged and buttery, with none of the haughty breeding of southern glasshouse blooms.

If this were a novel you would spend an afternoon picking them, picking them, hours and hours of gathering enough to strew, to cover thickly the bed, the sleeping bag, the pallet fit for a middle-heighted, middle-weighted woman to recline, and when you do, lie together, those flowers pressed against your skin will stain it with their Arctic ink, a bluish-black, the blood of permafrost. A bed of Arctic poppies on Ellesmere, and a lover to read their ink.

Oh Anna, you should have escaped to Ellesmere.

But Lake Hazen is a National Park (official) and you pick no flowers, only dream them as a passion for your reading. Tolstoy insisting that sex is dangerous: sexual desire an unleashed demon that should be controlled and organized, scripted and domesticated. In order to contain Anna's sexuality, Tolstoy must make her unhappy; she cannot enjoy her appetites as simply and enthusiastically as Stiva does. Anna's eroticism, the power she exerts, is culturally mis/timed, and she is damned. She has not appropriate colouration to suit the trappings of bourgeois respectability that first Karenin, then Vronsky, and above all Tolstoy, wish to impose on her. Her real sin is that she will not serve, and so old Tolstoy, he who claimed that she should be pitied rather than despised, is merciless and pitiless. He shadows her unto her death.

Hiking between the shadow hills. Flying over, it is possible to see them as harbingers of shadow, a dense purple-blue deeply buried within. Torn rifts of snow accentuate that shadow, its deep accompaniment. Chionophiles, those creatures highly adapted to snow. True chionophiles. Anna lacks the necessary camouflage, acclimatization, how can she endure that freezing scape? Chionophilitization takes practice, years of adaptment, and how could she accommodate herself, those dresses never gave her much protection, all struts and no insulation. Anna is shadowed past her seductions.

Shadow hills: the presence of shadows. *'If we have no one following us about like a shadow, it doesn't prove that we have the right to condemn her.'* Your favourite voice, the Princess Myagky. For all that she is allowed to exist on only eight pages of the novel, she enlists your complete attention, as if she were a companion reader. Princess Myagky, speaking plainly. Speaking plainly is an asset. Oh, she insists, with great courtesy, walking beside you (she grows more courteous as the landscape grows more desolate, as you trudge higher in your climb toward Glacier Pass), speaking plainly is much easier than all that double-double-talk, that determined pretending to be innocent when one has already buried the dagger in the topic's back. I speak too plainly. That's why he expunged me. He thought I would steal scenes from his precious contemplative Levin.

You laugh, but knowing that she is likely to take herself off over the next ridge, persist: But Anna's shadow – you mentioned it first. She looks for a moment crestfallen, even ashamed, as if she wishes she were not part of the book's society. She was followed by shadows, they were written into her part. Vronsky? Oh, he was only the obvious one, the physical translation of Anna's subversions. There were others. That fool of a husband, although everyone pretended to find him so clever. Her lubricious brother, with his chambermaids and governesses. Her precious son. Her damnable literary history. Her author. Her presumed status. Her age. Her sex. What they all forced her to represent. Indentured, she was.

Princess, you say, sliding your pack off and sitting down on a rock. You are offering me a theory of social conditioning for her behaviour. She sighs. You were asking about Anna's shadows. I am merely pointing out that she was a shadowed woman, and if we are so lucky as not to be pursued, then we have no right to condemn her. We too would succumb to a shadow were it to offer itself up, to follow us interminably. She gestures toward the shadow hills around us. Here there are shadows that are simply themselves, without any need to attach themselves to a person as either blessing or curse. Imagine, shadows that play with themselves all day, never needing to be entertained or put into a novel as a serious character. Shadows that are not authored or invented as metaphors, especially persistent male lovers who will pester a woman until she succumbs to her own damnable rebellion, her enforced destiny/curse. Far better to be a shadow, my dear, than a shadow's person.

If Anna needs seduction, Ellesmere will do. Not only the Arctic poppies yellowing the mornings but the steady wind and the rustle of the creeks braiding their paths down from the glaciers. Even hauling water is magnified pleasure, to kneel so at the edge of a rocky stream and clatter your small plastic bucket against the stones worn down by the very coldness of the water, and the water swirling to fill it so icy it hurts the teeth, the nose, the forehead when you drink. These are gestures lost in the city, lost on the platforms of railway stations, lost everywhere, the hand dipping a bucket into running water, lifting it from the shoulder and walking with that peculiar swing that balances the enclosure of its splash. Pleasure, seduction: buckets and water and stones and the muscles of shoulder and arm.

In the mornings the jaegers strut past. You feed them your

leftover pancakes, which they peck at judiciously, bright-eyed. They are gossipy, sociable, fly after and in front of you keeping company. They ensure the continued social order of Ellesmere, they watch for infidelities and ruptures, shake their heads warningly at Anna. If you sleep in they wake you, scrabbling on the tent cross. And then watch, quizzical and interested while you wash and cook and commit the human irreplaceables of coffee drinking and teeth brushing. And yet they would not exile her, ostracize her for choosing different alliances. Familiars, they defy Tolstoy and his inventions (those Madam Kartasovs) who believe it is a disgrace even to sit next to Anna.

Mornings are always brighter, the sun reaching a subtle intensity early (what there is of early and late) around four. That is when you wake, turn on your back and lie, looking up at the green-brown tent weave and the eerie quiet of the arctic night, wishing to stay; whispering aloud, Ellesmere, Ellesmere, the light passing over as slowly as the fugitive moss grows between the frost polygons and the gravel. The evenings shadow themselves, although there is the same sun, virtually, the same sun rotating the sky without interruption, careless of the compartmentalized determinations of public morality. Here Anna, there are no judgments exerting themselves, no old wives with their domestic tyrannies.

After your social rituals of setting up the tent, of water fetching and boiling, of coffee, after the splash of water on the face, when you have finally taken off your boots for the day, you lie looking down the valley of the glacial wash towards the lake, ice-puzzled still, the pieces caught in their own mysterious swatching. You open Anna. The book is getting dog-earred,

although you are pleased with Penguin: it has not started to fall
apart and it will not fall apart before the trip is over despite the
number of times you pull it from your pocket, despite the rain,
the dust, the bent corners. Every time you take it out, its
substance pleases you. Even the texture of the pages and the tiny
but sharp print, the elegant curve of the Js and the abrupt
triangle of the capital A – which recurs as a reminder of Anna
herself. Anna Arkadyevna. Such a sharp little pyramid of a name.
In this light, every letter, every word, is sharper than it reads
down south. Sometimes that stridence is unbearable and you
shove the book back into your pocket unable to withstand its
sheen, the gathering force of its numbered pages, Anna's
numbered days.

Every shadow shadows shadow. A shade cast upon different
light: rippled light upon a shade. Remnants, traces, darkenings.
The darkening skies of the north, its endless night impossible to
configure now in the steeped light of summer. In the distance,
Lake Hazen riffles through every version of blue. The first day it
is no more than a textured conglomeration of white, knobbled
ice butting against itself. Slow cracks, the blue between creep
imperceptibly every day wider, a stretching of the lazy water,
azure. The puzzle pieces are scattered farther, stirred apart on
the blue board of the lake by a huge finger of sun, still caught in
its implacable rotation, only slanting low between three and ten
before it describes an arc upwards again. Lake Hazen a carelessly
broken jigsaw abandoned after a lazy Sunday dinner. There are
huge sheets of ice left, almost square, and hundreds of tiny pieces
orbiting in endless float.

This ice picture: enigmatic, fascinating, a portrait of Anna

herself. Despite Levin and Kitty, despite Stiva and Dolly, it is
Anna who is irresistible, for whom you turn the pages. Despite
the larded and over-larded philosophizings of Levin, the billiard
games and travellings abroad, it is Anna you always see, off to
one side, perched on the edge of a stony tussock with her red bag
in her hand. Just as you always, from a rise, see the lake, can
watch it transfigure itself under its ever-changing cloak of ice.
The clothed lake, waterskin, sometimes a solid coat of white,
sometimes in rags and tatters, sometimes only wisps, faint
promises of ice returning. Here nothing melts, only the heart.
And the fleeting shadows.

Anna's shadow is written to be Vronsky. Or is it her
discontent, her lack of discipline? When you ask her, she nods
demurely, looking down at her quick, small hands, their gestures
so eloquent. A drawing room state of affairs, my dear, she says
sadly. Husbands and lovers are only and always creatures of
fiction. The truth is I wanted to step out of the house, and
Tolstoy allowed me, giving me fair warning, of course, that I
would suffer the consequences. Was I to blame? Her head is
lowered, perhaps against the glare of the sun, the endless light.
She fusses for a moment with the cuffs of her dress, the single
strand of pearls around her neck. Beside her, in your anorak and
boots, you catch yourself feeling clumsy, modern. And stop the
jolt of physical envy she arouses; you refuse to emulate other
women in their shunning. This Anna needs a friend, a woman
friend, a reader. She invites you to try on some of her clothes,
saying that you would particularly enjoy the green bombazine,
but you refuse and you don't even offer her yours. It is impossible
to imagine her shrugging into your t-shirt and jeans, your heavy
sweater and jacket. I've been invented this way, she says with a

light laugh. I cannot uninvent myself by dressing otherwise.

But whose invention is she? Tolstoy's? The nineteenth century's? Russia's? The novel's? Yours? She is the north's invention, her figure only dreamable when the eye swings towards the polar star. But how then to read her? Is it possible to read her in the south, from the south? In that blindly south-faced reading, is it possible to read at all? You are closer to Moscow than you are to Edmonton, to Edberg, to Calgary. You are closer to Russia than to home: reading is a new act here, not introverted and possessive but exploratory, the text a new body of self, the self a new reading of place. The closest you can get to Anna's Russia and still remain at home is this north; the closest you can get to home and still read Russia is this north; the closest you can get to reading and still know story is this undiscovered place: the farthest possible reach of all reaches, this island paradise, this un/written northern novel, this desert un/kingdom.

Free here of the graspings of most of [ ]man's impositions, his history or fiction or implacable des/scribement, [wo]men either real or invented. You can walk, sleep, read, within this pristine novel, waiting to be read, pleasure yourself in its open spine. This geograficione, this Ellesmere. You have read farther than there are pages, travelled farther than there are fictions. You are seduced, a lost woman, reading from within the fiction of all lost/damned/condemned/free women. Knowing that this story, all that is written, can be un/read, uninscribed. The words are stirred, mixed, like pieces of a jigsaw, broken up into their separate shapes and the whole picture lost, left to be recon- structed by another, a different hand.

Anna's hands. Small, fine, like her feet. And like her body, her hands hold things firmly, as if flesh has strength and does not need to excuse its presence, deny itself. Animation, radiance, nature, energy, all in her hands. Her strong little hands holding other hands, holding her own happiness. Anna puts her life into Vronsky's hands and reads her error, with her strong hands she holds fast. And Tolstoy punishes her for those strong little hands, their wilfullness, their pleasure. Having given them to her, he wants to take them back. Anna is amputated, headless and handless. The eroticism of Anna's hands: cut off.

What is never amputated is her shadow. Not Vronsky (only eliminated by Anna's elimination of herself), but the reading shadow, the head bent above the page: the peasant. Not the literal peasants that labour cheerfully through the novel, eating and drinking and working, giving earthy advice and acting as deterministic models for Levin (who requires models for work and belief, for sleep and love and even habit – why do you dislike Levin so much: his pomposity, his self-importance?), but the nemesis peasant, the ominous little man who shovels his way into the novel at the wrong moments, a heart-stopping apparition. You speculate that this peasant is Tolstoy (who would enjoy using that guise to visit his reading) interfering in his own text, refusing to permit you to read without intrusion, Tolstoy an impatient passenger in his own conveyance: *a peasant carrying a sack over his shoulder*. Who will not take proper precautions, who cannot wait to jump off the train, abandon Anna to its track. The peasant as dyslexic reader, stooped and muttering, sometimes in French and sometimes in Russian. In the sack over his shoulder is the novel, a huge muddle of words into which he stuffs the cut-off hands of beautiful expressive women who refuse to be domestic. The peasant who moves *like an ox with bent head*, Karenin himself hauling the sack of his bureaucratic incomprehension. Levin's literal peasants competing with this figurative peasant who lumbers around with the novel smothered in his sack, a sack that he shakes up as if it contains pieces of a puzzle or lottery tickets. The peasant beater the omen of big train endings, reading the text of wheels and rails before their ominous conjunction with flesh, the deterministic writer herding his characters toward an eternally shunting goods train.

The peasant is the un/reader of the presence of passion. It is he who assigns passion the potential for destruction, he stuffs both good and bad children into his nightmare, he trundles off the remains of both excellent and mediocre dinners, he mutters and bends and hammers. The peasant as meddlesome, moralistic, terrifying writer. The first off the train, the last on the train, the last character to register on Anna, her abandonment.

Levin idealizes and romanticizes the peasant. What do you expect? He wants to authorize himself as peasant in order to put all possible Annas in their possible places. He is happy with Kittys, sweet, thoughtless girls who preoccupy themselves with cooking jam and household inventories. (And why are you so irritated with Kitty: is it her penchant for cooking, for bustling about, for her scripted life set up to implement Levin's vision? Her obedience? No wonder she goes looking for thunderstorms and bolts of lightning.) Levin and the meaningful peasant interchangeable. The worst nightmare for character or novel would be to wake and find that she was being stuffed into the mouth of that black paunch.

Why is Vronsky never stuffed into the peasant sack? Why does Tolstoy permit him society, dignity? He can go out and about as he pleases; he is never publicly humiliated (except when he falls off his horse). His property and his mother and his self-satisfaction do not diminish. He has *other interests*: ambition, self-advancement, a predilection for the hedonistic. Nineteenth century Russian society be damned, you believe that Tolstoy could give *him* a few moments of misery. The most that Tolstoy punishes him is in forcing him to take care of the green cucumber, that visiting prince sampling the wares of the world and whom Vronsky is delegated to entertain.

> *The prince enjoyed unusually good health even for a prince. Thanks to athletics and training he was so physically fit that in spite of the excesses he indulged in when taking his pleasures he looked as fresh as a big shiny green Dutch cucumber. The prince had travelled a great deal, and in his opinion one of the chief advantages of the modern facilities of communication was that they made the delights of all nations accessible.*

Vronsky is uncomfortable because in the prince he sees the worst of himself, but that is as close as Tolstoy comes to pushing Vronsky toward the peasant/capturer.

Still, after days of entertaining the green cucumber with as much disreputable disreputation as possible, Vronsky dreams about his peasant/writer's potential reading of the story.

> *...memories of the disreputable scenes he had witnessed during the last few days became confused and merged with a mental image of Anna and of a peasant who had played an important part as a beater in the bear-hunt; and Vronsky fell asleep. He awoke in the dark, trembling with horror, and hurriedly lighted a candle. 'What was it? What was the dreadful thing I dreamed? Yes, I know. The peasant-beater – a dirty little man with a matted beard – was stooping down doing something, and all of a sudden he began muttering strange words in French. Yes, there was nothing else in the dream,' he said to himself. 'But why was it so awful?' He vividly recalled the*

peasant again and the incomprehensible French words the man had muttered, and a chill of horror ran down his spine.

So terrifying the incomprehensible "French" of the writer as he beats his characters into plowshares, or into railway ties, or their potential deaths. The writer no aristocrat of words shedding light on a human gesture, but a rather grubby labourer muttering and incomprehensible, engaged in some horrifying act of violation, a sinister blacksmith/rapist.

He rummages in Anna's bedroom, in the secret precincts of her passionate world.

> *'I dreamed that I ran into my bedroom to fetch something or find out something – you know how it is in dreams,' she said, her eyes wide with horror. 'And in the bedroom, in the corner, stood something.'*
>
> *'Oh, what nonsense! How can you believe...'*
>
> *But she would not let him interrupt. What she was saying was too important to her.*
>
> *'And the something turned round, and I saw it was a peasant with a tangled beard, little and dreadful-looking. I wanted to run away, but he stooped down over a sack and was fumbling about in it with his hands...'*
>
> *She showed how he had fumbled in the sack. There was terror in her face. And Vronsky, remembering his own dream, felt the same terror fill his being.*
>
> *'And all the time he was rummaging, he kept muttering very quickly in French, you know, rolling his rs: Il faut le battre, le fer; le broyer, le pétrir...And I was so terrified I tried to wake up...and I did wake up but it was still part of the dream.'*

"It must be beaten, must the iron, pound it, knead it." The writer beating his character into submission, the very text alien to her, her story. The fiction impossible to read, stuffed into a gunnysack, rummaged, constantly searched, fumbled, a kind of physical ransacking. In the same way is Anna rummaged, fumbled, groped by Tolstoy, her passions and inclinations jumbled together in his gunnysack, roughly thrown over the shoulder and carted on an extended pilgrimage to represent the fate of wayward women. This is pity? Once in a while in the long journey, the peasant puts the bag on the ground and fumbles inside, determined to beat the uncompromising female sensibility within into some semblance of a tool or an instrument.

You feel sick. You shove the book aside and try to rest your eyes on the ice-float lake, on an Arctic hare that jogs its lazy way along the grassy stream edge. She hasn't got a hope, you knew it all along, but somehow this is worse, this knowing you are reading her usage, a witness to Tolstoy's assault, even if not his intention. Does he intend to be kind to her, does he intend to show and disagree with the enforced exile of women who disturb? Or, having written her, does he then refuse to *read* her, imposing the death sentence that was written into her before she offered herself for reading? You shudder to think of being read by such a man, of your life/places drawn into such static circum-scription. You know you are a character in a larger novel, a novel of geography and passion, reading yourself as you are being read by a comprehensive reader. How would this reading read your places, your self written between habitations, the braille of fingers on each locational inflection?

But far down the bank, in a flash so swift you could imagine them running past their own running, you catch the race of a small herd of Peary caribou. They are unrestrained, joyous and gone. If your notice had wandered, if you hadn't been trying to read an answer to Anna, they would have passed your mutual landscape unread. If no one sees them, are they there? It is a gift: you lift your pack again knowing it is possible to run free, escape the boundaries of page or place, their constraints. They perform beneficence: a caribou beat across the unread tundra to remind you that you can un/read her, free her from her written self, read self, punished self.

Anna interprets her dream to mean that she will die in childbirth, and in truth she dies in birth, caught in the birth canal: the impossible woman who wants more than either the writer or his place will permit her to have. The peasant/writer/ Tolstoy is not so much beating her into a plowshare as raping her, which she understands in a subsequent dream, although the act is obfuscated for the reader.

> At dawn a horrible nightmare, which she had had several times even before her connexion with Vronsky, repeated itself and woke her. A little old man with unkempt beard was leaning over a bar of iron, doing something and muttering meaningless words in French, and – this was what always made the nightmare so horrible – she felt that though this peasant seemed to be paying no attention to her he was doing something dreadful to her with the iron. She awoke in cold perspiration.

Not Vronsky who does Anna in but Tolstoy, he the peasant who severs/penetrates her with the iron, a symbolic but obviously sexual attack: exactly as Tolstoy annihilates Anna for her sexual nature. The same peasant muttering the same incomprehensible foreign language grinds Anna beneath the freight cars of the train. In her final reading of the world, when everything seems grimy and distorted, the peasant reappears. Anna prevented from reading a future for herself – her obvious difference and her interest in her own story altered by her creator – and now she reads everything as hideous, vile, foolish and affected.

> To avoid seeing people she got up quickly and seated herself at the opposite window of the empty compartment. A grimy, deformed-looking peasant in a

cap from beneath which tufts of his matted hair stuck out, passed by this window, stooping down to the carriage wheels. 'There's something familiar about that deformed peasant,' thought Anna. And remembering her dream, she walked over to the opposite door, trembling with fright.

Anna is right to be afraid: Tolstoy is about to beat her into a railway tie, rape her with her own reading. His forced and enforced writing of Anna will crush her beneath the cars of the text she has travelled for so many pages. Anna the reader un/read into her own un/doing: her own extinction and extinguishment.

Anna carrying her little red purse, only too obviously the red purse of her cunt, its secret wealth of pleasure. So poignant its colour, its presence there, thrown aside before she, the red envelope of her self, is thrown aside. The red bag that she carries, her vitality, her imagination, her rebellions apart from her creator, thrown aside. Her medicine bundle, her heart, the heart that beats so quickly, quickly, before she destroys the woman that her writer insisted on writing to the bitter end, Anna the reader profoundly out/distancing his closure. Anna, removed instantly to deserts and islands, to potential Ellesmeres.

And exactly at the moment when the space between the wheels drew level with her she threw aside the red bag and drawing her head down between her shoulders dropped on her hands under the truck, and with a light movement, as though she would rise again at once, sank on to her knees. At that same instant she became horror-struck at what she was doing. 'Where am I? What am I doing? Why?' She tried to get up, to throw herself back; but something huge and relentless struck her on the head and dragged her down on her back. 'God forgive me everything!' she murmured, feeling the impossibility of struggling. A little peasant muttering something was working at the rails. And the candle by which she had been reading the book filled with trouble and deceit, sorrow and evil, flared up with a brighter light, illuminating for her everything that before had been enshrouded in darkness, flickered, grew dim and went out forever.

Tolstoy, that muttering peasant, working the rails. Everything reads Tolstoy writing Anna toward a monstrous rape, his resolution to the woman who should be "pitied rather than despised." What then, in all of Ellesmeres, can you do?

Remove her to the land of light. On Ellesmere, the light shines with a blue haze that Anna remembers from happy days before her life was subject to the determinations of men. '*I remember that blue haze, like the haze on the mountains in Switzerland,*' says Anna, of the pleasurable desires of youth. In the evening, its cold ether wraps hands around you, you look down to Lake Hazen as if you have decamped to the realms of terra incognita. From here it is impossible to read the world: the world exists only in some enigmatic novel far beyond this sky, this dome of green, this stony ground, the glaciers you are trekking toward. In a never/read text, you lose the text of your usual fictions. Words speak a different weight. Your feet resemble only faintly the feet you walk in Calgary, that walked from Edberg to Edmonton and on, despite their mileage, despite their obvious physical connexion to you. Ellesmere un/reading. The trains that shunt Anna back and forth between Moscow and Petersburg, between Russia and the countries of Europe, could not conceive of how to traverse Ellesmere. No amount of hammering could shape this floating woman/island into a metal bar. Within this endless light, she resists all earlier reading.

You wade the Abbé River too, and again the force, the surge of electricity in the water makes you want simply to submerge yourself into a tumbled stone. You want to become Ellesmere. But traverse on, puzzle-ice in the lake you can still see as you go higher, and the tussocks you step over eternity of continuance. The same principle: jumping from moment to moment across an abrupted space. Stepping stones cross lewdly noisy creeks. August a place of unreading. You walk. You stop. You drink cold water. You rummage in your pack. You wake to light. You sleep to light. The light lights and lightens. The sky burns, the wind rises and dies. No preconditioned reading. No dark, no flaring then snuffed-out candle. When you leave Hazen camp, you tell Bezal when you plan to be back, the number of days. "As long as you get back before dark," he says, with his wry smile.

There is no dark. You read all night.

Anna has never been read so well, you will un/read her reading, this Anna as scarlet woman cast into the outer darkness of moral turpitude, of blame, a site of sin. Anna written as serially wrong: wrong to want to extricate herself from the unfortunate Karenin (his ears, his cracking knuckles), wrong to love passionately, wrong to want her child, her writer writing her into wrong-doing until she is un/done by that writing. This is the moral weight that Anna bears, that crushes her. Created by a man, written by a man, read by men, revised by men; now, here on Ellesmere, you dare to set her free from the darkness of pages, her horrid shadow. Anna written as victim, trapped by convention's implacable refusals, a woman who gives up everything for love, destroys herself and everyone around her. Contradictions of loss and selfishness that write her into the very kneeling position she emblematically occupies: supplicant, irretrievably lost, crushed between the industrial force of the two train cars. Adulteress, sinner, deviant, morally bankrupt, with only her little red bag as company.

Tolstoy sets her up, the initial Anna so full of vitality and energy, so easily able to fire the blood of those who connect with her. Turns on her, changes her from that vibrant body to a vamp. And then, even worse, he's pissed off for her indefensible position, imposes childishness and jealousy, spends the rest of the novel writing her as having failed him. You always suspected this, but now you are certain.

Terror of women = terror of the north. Lost in one frozen waste or another, lost to women or the wiles of Ellesmere.

Reading in this clear green light an act different from reading south under the sanctimonious permission of fluorescent and incandescent fixtures. Reading changed by the quality of light it partakes of, the shadows it endures. Here the only shadow that of your body, whether you are sitting on a rock or stretched full-length in your sleeping bag, your toes curling with their own pleasure, propped on an elbow as you turn the thin pages following Anna's impossible infatuation.

At first you accept the dominant reaction, want to shake her, send her to reform class for erring wives. Stop it, Anna, Vronsky's not worth it; you will end up in a morgue. But you see his ears, Karenin's ears. She's right, the man is intolerable. He refuses to have plastic surgery and only pure stubbornness prevents him from recognizing his own ungainly features. Cartilage, he is all cartilage, and what is worse, he doesn't even know it himself. How the hell could anyone, critic, reader, Tolstoy, the sternest moralist, expect a woman as alive as Anna to stay with a man of such terrible cartilage. If Tolstoy is going to get so damned moralistic about her lapse, then he shouldn't give Karenin such ears. Ears like that, holding apart such a supercilious head, bent below the edge of his hat, are publicly liable for what they provoke. The ear bears seed; this organ is supposed to maintain equilibrium, keep balance, but Karenin's ears would drive any woman to take lovers. Plural. Many lovers, a raft of them, a desportment of lovers, and the institution of marriage to a man with such ears be damned.

As you hike around the shoulder of Varsity Mountain, all you can see are Karenin's ears, in a particular way – from the back. His haircut is very high, militarily close, although Vronsky is the military man, not Karenin.

> *'But why is it his ears stick out so oddly? Or has he had his hair cut too short?'*

Women who take lovers might offer potential treatises on their husbands' ears. These are the short railway journeys between one action and another: not moral corruption or a violation of social codes. One moment his ears are tolerable; the next they simply are not. You understand this perfectly, which does not make you – or Anna for that matter – frivolous. The ear bespeaks the whole.

The ears of Ellesmere lie beautifully folded, flat back against the head of the island. They curl in quiet listening, they are comely as conch-shells, as seductive as the small gurgles of the many streams, the mossy tussocks growing out of permafrost. Surely in winter the wind would make any ear hear – acutely, the keening of a northern distinction. From here, it is easier to hear Russia than to hear the railways of lower Canada. Over the continental shelf and down its slope, under the mountains below the permanent ice cap of the polar sea, past Lomonosov Ridge, the Pole Plain and the Fram Basin, Nansen Ridge and the

Nansen Basin, the Svyataya Anna Fan, there, there past
Komsomolets Island, is the long sweep of Siberia, calling. These
un/read islands, these Annas all. Inexplicable, these northerns
belong to no nation, no configuration of [wo]man. They are
Annas, impossible to possess, determined to enact their own
vitality.

Anna needs to see Karenin (his slightly rounded back, his
sarcasm, his tired eyes): out of her determinedly married self read
herself anew. That is what Vronsky does for her, not because he
is so marvellous but because there appears with him the
possibility of a new story; Anna can invent herself in an
undocumented landscape, an undetermined fiction. That is the
temptation Tolstoy holds out to her.

Along the river toward Gilman Graben and Glacier Pass you
climb, climb. Although you have used some food and fuel, your
packs weigh heavy and the shale burns through your boots. It is
the Garfield Range you are climbing, not that high actually, but
climbing, climbing. Across Lake Hazen you can see the mouth of
the Ruggles River, the braided-stream mouth of the Abbé distant
and below. Visibility: the Abbé Glacier shining turquoise. And
always Lake Hazen, every mood of its water and ice daily broken
into greater open, the wind from the south blowing the chill
mouth of the Agassiz icecap toward you. Invisible but felt, back-
packing mammals moving with upright slowness across the shale
against the red-rich mountainside, your grey-green tent a tiny
hump shouldering boundless space. Not empty, but full of breath
and plenitude, the portentous coming of snow, soon now. Siberia
is never far away: visible just over the horizon.

Annas are always too visible: demand visibility as women

determined to enact their own moments in the world. They are watched, judged, condemned. Annas carry the weight of Siberia, even if they are not sent there. And this Anna is indocile, perverse, dangerously wilful, at least in the readings of the men she shares fiction with. Such public indiscretion just for the love of Vronsky? The mistake men make is in thinking that such women commit public indiscretions for love. Improprieties for love? Or improprieties enacted as an expression of a desire for freedom?

From Karenins everywhere, the Karenin of the ears the same Karenin who engages the moth-hunting lawyer. You read him with laughter, he brings a breath of slapstick rapaciousness to the novel, a vignette to compete with the Princess Myagky. When Anna rejects the *honourable protection of his name*, Karenin resorts to a legalistic reading of the social law he is no longer chief bureaucratic instrument of. His wife, Anna, is part of the portfolio he carries under his arm, tightly squeezed against his side by an implacable elbow; and if she will not remain in his husband's portfolio he will find a lawyer to put her in another. The famous Petersburg lawyer is always busy; he keeps everyone waiting. They are all caught in a waiting room without a book to read, while the lawyer keeps a battery of clerks to write and re/write his nasty tomes. He the caricature of the upwardly mobile writer who would like to write women into legal and historical place.

> The lawyer was a short, thick-set, bald-headed man, with a dark, reddish beard, fair bushy eyebrows, and a prominent forehead. He was as spruce as a bridegroom, from his necktie and double watch-chain to his patent-leather boots. He had a clever, rustic face, while his clothes were dandified and in bad taste.

The lawyer stands in for all husbands wishing to keep their wives in bondage, he is eternal bridegroom, their perpetual substitute. But as writer and reader of story, he is barbarian, a killer. Ensconced behind his desk, he reveals himself a kind of body-snatcher.

'Won't you sit down?' He indicated an arm-chair by the writing-table stacked with papers, and ensconced himself behind the desk, rubbing his little hands together with their short fingers covered with white hairs, and bending his head to one side. But hardly had he settled down before a moth flew over the table. The lawyer, with a swiftness that could never have been expected of him, caught the moth between his hands, and resumed his former attitude.

Karenin's ears; the lawyer's fingers. You read a place where husbands and their trappings are grotesque. Pretending to be listeners, they trap and crush, killers dressed as bridegrooms, their reassurances of secrecy and confidence dust jackets for confinement. The pleasure the Petersburg lawyer takes in his obscene readings of the law articulated by his delighted moth-catching.

The lawyer looked down at Karenin's feet, feeling that the sight of his overwhelming pleasure might offend his client. He glanced at a moth that flew past his nose, and put out a hand to catch it, but refrained out of respect for Karenin's position.

The lawyer's recitation of grounds for divorce as orchestrated as the short lives of moths: physical defect, desertion, adultery subdivided into its various components of mutual agreement or involuntary detection. He licks his lips on the latter, with its potential for a camera, a paid witness, a broken-down door. The lawyer is ruthless, malicious, prurient: he does well in fiction and in life.

And Tolstoy makes Anna a moth. Does he? Can he? An entire novel contrived to show her as a moth caught and crushed in an iron grip, an insistence that this is her fate. Tolstoy writing out the density of more than eight hundred pages to show her thus, and yet, and yet, you know that somehow she escapes his chill legalism, refuses to be dismissed as a flighty woman attracted to flame.

The insects on Ellesmere are small and torpid. Although in the heat of day the mosquitoes come out, they fly more than bite, seem to bunt and stagger when they approach human skin, as if they find it impossible to sink their teeth. They buzz the patches of flowers, climb the blue air, caught in their brief season.

You happen to witness the Princess Myagky and the Petersburg lawyer arguing. They have run into each other on the same patch of shale and one refuses to stand aside for the other. The princess finds him vulgar, but she will conquer him because she is less devious, she recognizes his amusement at everyone else's discomfort. You ought not, she tells him, make your fortune out of other people's shadows. But madame, he says suavely, believing himself charming, I do not invent their shadows. They create them themselves. I only detonate them. He kneels to polish his patent-leather boots with a yellow handkerchief. The toes are badly cut from the rock, from your journey toward the glacier. He catches a lazy mosquito in his fist, smiles as he crushes his fingers together. The Karenin case was not my fault. And it was never resolved, you know. I was never sure whether or who actually wanted the divorce, first Karenin insisting and Anna desisting, then Anna requesting and Karenin withholding. Very interesting paperwork that makes for! The Princess glares as if she would like to snatch his protruding forehead and squeeze it between her bottle-green gloves. And no one is responsible, she says dejectedly, for Anna being snuffed out, Anna dead in her desire to be free of those insufferable writs and notations, commentaries and observations. She chose that train because she was sick of being held morally responsible, of being snubbed, of being held up as an example, of being deemed a sinner by all those myriad [ ]men reading and commenting on her case for more than a hundred years. She does herself in because she is thoroughly sick, sick of herself. Her character renouncing all she is induced to represent. Those social circles she has to cope with, first as member and then as outcast. She's just plain tired! The lawyer snaps at a mosquito. She should know the consequences of what she does, he says and smiles grimly.

Going up toward Glacier Pass you encounter muskoxen feeding in a stream draw. They look at you watchfully, unafraid, lowering over the rise. Two-legged creatures slight threat. They snort as if warning you to keep your distance, small humped beasts like racks of bones, their hair now shaggy, tearing itself loose in patches, their summer moult. Unsociable they seem, but strangely moving, adapted to the inhospitable country here, to their harsh survival in cold and darkness. Later, you come across one alone, chewing with strange delicacy in a meadow of flowers. Bob inches closer and closer, wants a picture as close as space will allow. The huge horns lower, the head tosses, nostrils flare. Casually, aware of his own rights, he takes a short but definite run after you. No close-ups, no pictures, no pin-ups. So beautifully ugly, his desire for privacy here in this private place. Humans should study muskoxen, their solitary waywardness, the forbidden intimacies of horns and hair and shaggy face, the humped back of resilience. Waiting for snow, for darkness, for inevitable north to return.

You are caught between Anna and Ellesmere. Walking this landscape, indifferent, beyond beauty, toward the remote seat of the glacier you want to reach, the Abbé Glacier and the Seven Sisters frozen into their own eternities, high and remote, without the need to insist on emancipation or escape, themselves escaped into nordic dreams of extremity that permit you to wander here, carelessly, for a short space. Ellesmere teaches pleasure, the pleasure of oblivion, pleasure endorsed, its doors thrown wide. In the tent at night/day, you wake, turn to stare up at the woven cloth above you, the ground under your thermarest below your sleeping bag as knotty and firm as all facts. This is pleasure: escape, water, wind, air, rocks, the lake still frozen in the distance behind you, the potential of glacial ice and snow, of always reading an eternal book, of Anna reading this book you are in, this book of the north, un/read because mysterious, this female desert island and its secret reasons and desires.

The day you return from the glacier, you realize that Anna is condemned because she reads.

You are astonished to discover this in the novel, waiting there, your own addiction so carefully prepared for on this trip where you have lost libraries and bookstores, where only the jaegers and the arctic hares bounce between lines. Your pages flutter in the wind that funnels from the glaciers above, from the glaciers to the north, from Russia just over the flat top of the world. The strange phenomenon of horizon: in certain light and at certain times it flattens itself so that you can see past the horizon, over the horizon, beyond it. Looming. It is a trick of light and of the latitude here, the extremity of north. A reading ahead, the potential of all readers for reading ahead, skipping before and over the words to find out what happens before it happens. That is what Anna does: she reads ahead of herself.

Arguments in the novel about the emancipation of women: jocular resolutions. You want to punch them all: Tolstoy and Vronsky and Karenin and Levin. The dangers of educating women: they'll know too much, become uncontrollable, then what is to be done with them? And are they fit for the serious duties of men: jurymen, telegraph clerks, witnesses? Nobody in those drawing rooms speaks of freedom.

Women reading/distracted from domestic duties. Anna reads too much. Anna reads more than anyone in the novel (except perhaps Levin). What she reads is more of a mystery than Levin's always laid-out and pondered reading. Reading gets Anna into trouble, makes her want to understand herself, read herself rather than live heedlessly between girlhood and courtship and wifehood and motherhood and eternal domesticity. Anna's desire to be her own text emblematic of her desire for control. She will not be read except she be un/read, and only love or the passionate reader can do that for her, not moralistic and sharp-nosed critics who evaluate/weigh/judge her, find her so much wanting.

You need a book for Ellesmere. Anna needs books. You read her because she reads: Tolstoy is blind interpreter. Did he know the woman he was writing, could her *read* her? You must free her from the constraints of the novel she has been imprisoned in, shake her loose from the pages of her own story so that she can float over the landscape here in this landscape of a woman, this northern body, waiting to fall in love. You are in love with

Ellesmere. You are in love with your hiking boots, with the ache in the small of your back, with your battered pack. When you turn your hand over and look at it, you are choked with love for your own frail body, the way it bends and moves, its muscles, its quiet aging, the lines it draws on itself. It takes its own readings, quietly, while you take its story for granted.

When Anna is first offered, she seems as thoughtless as all other women, talking endlessly about her son with Vronsky's mother who is talking endlessly about her son. Sons as determiners of mothers as determiners of stories as determiners of morals. Then Anna meets Vronsky. Her behaviour even sillier, all that flirting and dancing for him (although you shouldn't be surprised, given Karenin's ears). Vronsky is a nice body, a pair of boots and legs, a smiling mouth, two hands, decent ears. Pleasant, handsome, affable. Impossible that he would alter any life, certainly not the life of an Anna. But he offers Anna a good read, just as now women might look for a potentially good lay, that too a song suggestive in its need for audience.

Vronsky introduces Anna to the potential for story. Once he is there, on the scene, Anna begins to read: you read about her reading. The real novel (about Anna reading) begins, it is about you reading Anna, it is about all Annas and their readings of themselves. Here, on Ellesmere, you see now how reading is an alien act, such a strange activity beside the daily motions of sleeping and eating and fetching water and walking, of tilting your head to look at the sky, of stopping to rest. Only the north can teach what reading means, and you are a woman in the north, reading a woman written by a man to whom women were a mystery, a man who did not know what Anna was reading, who pushed her from one side of the book to the other, interfering, manipulative. A northern: *un*read Anna. On the train back to Petersburg after she has met Vronsky, danced, flirted with him, then, worried, decided to go home, Anna begins to read her own story. She is on her way back to her ordinary life, but her gestures have changed.

Still in the same worried frame of mind in which she had been all day, Anna arranged herself with pleasure and deliberation for the journey. With small, deft hands she opened a red bag and took out a little cushion, which she laid on her knees before relocking the bag. Then she carefully wrapped a rug round her legs and sat down again. An invalid lady had already settled herself for the night. Two other ladies began talking to Anna, and a stout old woman tucked up her feet and remarked upon the heating of the train. Anna said a few words in reply, but, not foreseeing any entertainment from the conversation, asked Annushka to get a lamp, hooked it on to the arm of her seat, and took a paper-knife and an English novel from her bag.

Let the novel begin.

There would be nothing for you to read here on Ellesmere if Anna were to go back to her nice, everyday life. She would be the conventionally boring woman, acceptable to Karenin and Levin, inaccessible to Vronsky; despite her body's vitality and her laughing eyes, she would not exist. But she reads – English novels. And so, Anna will not subside into a woman who talks about her children, she will not subside into the carefully wrapped invalid or the stout old woman. Although her first desire is to read, she is distracted, perhaps because she is placed on that train by Tolstoy, and you know that he uses trains to displace her.

At first she made no progress with her reading. For a while the bustle of people coming and going was disturbing. Then, when the train had started, she could not help listening to the noises. Then the snow beating against the window on her left and sticking to the pane, the guard passing by muffled up and one side of him covered with snow, together with conversation about the terrible blizzard raging outside – all this distracted her attention.

Anna is travelling to Ellesmere; she needs to be transported there in order to read her English/Russian story. There is the incipient snow of the north, the blizzard hovering outside the window of the brief ecosummer permitted here in the extreme arctic. There is the muffled guard, a muskox passing.

And there, despite the world, is the novel. The novel you are reading on Ellesmere, the end of the world and the beginning of all reading and hence all worlds.

And so it went on: the same jolting and knocking, the same snow on the window, the same sudden transition from steaming heat to cold and back again to heat, the same glimpses of the same faces in the semi-darkness, and the same voices, and Anna began to read and to keep her mind on what she read. Annushka was already dozing, her broad hands in their gloves, one of which was split, clutching the red bag on her lap. Anna read attentively but there was no pleasure in reading, no pleasure in entering into other people's lives and adventures. She was too eager to live herself. If she read how the heroine of the novel nursed a sick man, she wanted to be moving about the sick-room with noiseless tread herself; if she read of a member of Parliament making a speech, she wanted to be delivering that speech herself; if she read how Lady Mary rode to hounds and teased her sister-in-law and astonished everyone by her daring – she would have liked to do the same. But there was no possibility of doing anything, so she forced herself to read, while her little hands twisted the smooth paper-knife.

Anna reads. She reads the story she would like to be living, and in that wish to partake of all the forbidden worlds of the novel, she abandons her position as good, everyday woman. The novel reads her past her limited world, enables her to long for action, to be able to *do*. Karenin does not lose Anna to Vronsky; he loses Anna to a novel. Anna's reading on the train is the story of herself, a woman who does not sit passively, talking of her children and waiting to arrive at a male destination, but a woman who acts, passionately, who *astonished everyone by her daring.*

Reading persists as the most dangerous activity any character can engage in. If Anna had never read her husband's ears so well, she might have been able to interrupt the path of her larger story. If Vronsky had been able to read his little mare better, he wouldn't have broken her back. If Karenin had had the imagination to perceive that Anna's reading might be different from his own, he could have saved his marriage. When Anna's novel is opened, Karenin tries to slam the book shut. But worse is the moment when he does read, with great intensity, Anna's face during that race Vronsky loses. It is the first and only time Karenin reads his wife. But already she is such a closed book to him that he cannot believe what her pages dis/cover; he even dares suggest that the text of her behaviour is unbecoming. By that time, Anna, wrapped up in her novel, does not give a damn.

When Anna takes the book out of her red bag, she frees her sexuality and she is lost. She will not stop reading until it is over.

> *And the candle by which she had been reading the book filled with trouble and deceit, sorrow and evil, flared up with a brighter light, illuminating for her everything that before had been enshrouded in darkness.*

She is understandably fascinated by her own story, but her reading in the darkness is Tolstoy's representation. She reads her way toward Ellesmere, where you will read her, where she has never been read before, you are willing to wager that uniqueness, where in perpetual daylight you un/read Tolstoy's reading of her reading.

Anna cannot escape darkness. You cannot escape light. She reads. You read. Vronsky peripheral to Anna's reading, yet part of the impossible novel she chooses to enter, to live within. She has opened her book and there he is, one of the characters. Entering fiction, Anna no longer content to sit back and watch everyone else doing; she reads her own actions and is dissatisfied with her previously unread life, Karenin's ears only the first of it. Anna reads so much that by the end of the novel she develops myopia. When Dolly sees her at Vozdvizhenskoe (reminding Dolly of an English novel's luxury), Anna has a new habit of screwing up her eyes. Anna has become near-sighted (you'll go blind) from all her reading. At Vozdvizhenskoe Anna rides (sexually). Anna as avid reader is no longer content to drive in sleepy carriages, to be driven by sleepy footmen, Tolstoy's illegitimacies. She will ride herself, control the read herself, even if it is a ride that breaks her back.

You carry glasses, contact lenses, the accoutrements of your habit. Reading enablements. Near-sighted, you can see nothing of Ellesmereland without glasses, need corrective lenses to unread both yourself and the myopic text.

Vronsky embodies textual opportunity for Anna. Merging her life with his, she reads more and more. She knows that her life as a fiction will end, but her reading is constant, she is source, text and the reading act itself.

> ...she spent a great deal of her time reading, both novels and such serious literature as was in fashion. She ordered all the books favourably reviewed in the foreign papers and magazines she took in, and applied herself to them with a concentration possible only in seclusion. She also made a special study,

from books and technical journals, of every subject of interest to Vronsky, so
that he frequently went straight to her with problems relating to agriculture
or architecture, and sometimes even horse-breeding or sport. He was amazed
at her knowledge and her memory, and was at first incredulous and inclined
to ask for confirmation of her facts. She would then find what he asked for in
some book, and show it him.

Although Vronsky doubts her reading, Anna makes herself well
read in an attempt to unread her earlier passivity. Tolstoy chafes
at Anna's reading, claiming she is still mainly preoccupied with
herself, but Anna's reading is more than simply emblematic,
more than simply time filled in.

The passion with which Anna flings herself into Vronsky is
similar to the passion with which she reads. He offers her the
opportunity of a living book, an act of imagination in an age
when an educated woman and a woman riding a horse are
similarly perverse, Anna's reading is her act of educating herself,
reading herself into an unreading of how she has been read.
More notable: Anna writes. Oblonsky claims she is writing a
children's book, but it is clear that what Anna is doing when
Tolstoy is not looking is writing herself, and the Anna who reads
is a front for the Anna writing her own passionate involvement
with her own story.

What you are unreading here on Ellesmere is not so much an
Anna in love or an Anna in misguided passion, but an Anna in
imagination, unwilling to limit herself to the role of mournfully
wrongful victim and adulteress. Anna's fear is her fear that
imagination will end, she will be destitute. Vronsky is all she has.
Anna's reading of him is the novel she is immersed in. Her
jealousy of him is jealousy of her reading. She must question all
fictions (especially Vronsky's) because she is jealous of the story,

which is essentially hers.

> *She laid her hands on his shoulders, and gave him a long, searching look, her eyes full of love. She was studying his face, making up for the time she had not seen him, comparing, as she did every time they met, the picture of him in her imagination (incomparably superior, impossible in reality) with him as he actually was.*

The Vronsky Anna loves is the one her imagination reads.

And Anna reads her own death well in advance of its happening; even before she leaves Karenin, she knows how she will come to the end of her story. Anna has only to imagine her death to read it clearly.

> *'Death!' she thought. And such horror fell upon her that for a long while she could not make out where she was, and her trembling hands could not find a match with which to light another candle in the place of the one that had burned low and gone out.*

The darkness that finally extinguishes Anna's reading light is the island of her own imagination, inventing the unexpected life of a woman who belongs to herself. She will extinguish her lamp when she pleases.

> *And the candle by which she had been reading the book filled with trouble and deceit, sorrow and evil, flared up with a brighter light, illuminating for her everything that before had been enshrouded in darkness, flickered, grew dim and went out for ever.*

But not quite for ever. Here in the forever light of Ellesmere you are unreading the Anna that Tolstoy pretended to write. He killed her off: she closed the book. He writes her an adulteress; she falls in love with her imagination.

After Anna's death, Vronsky's mother claims that Anna's desperate passions were *'all for the sake of being original.'* Vronsky's mother the classically condemning, socially punitive woman/ reader, speaking the unknown truth. Yes, Anna enacts an original life, lives the creativity of a woman in a frozen land, with only one book to read or to write, her very only, very own life.

So you think this novel unbecoming for a woman? Ellesmere is no one's mistress. Every day you slide your legs out of your sleeping bag, unzip the tent and look up at the sky, privileged to be reading its story for a while, the pages of wind and glacier, of arctic silence, Ellesmere's book unpossessible. You will have to abandon it here when you leave, for the hares and caribou. In the crisp air, pulling on your socks, then your shoes before you walk over a ridge to pee, down to the creek to splash water on your face, you read a passionate woman floating in the arctic ocean beyond the reach of all interference, all authors and bookings.

Anna Arkadyevna and Ellesmere. Karenin erased, not even smart enough to see the famous traveller, just returned from China, who is now on his way to northern Canada as the next exotic stop. Vronsky enlisted, headed for the Serbian war against the Turks, with a toothache. Kitty and Dolly Tolstoy's puppets, good girls, parables. Tolstoy running away from his own story into another story.

Reader and Anna and Ellesmere. She sits on a large stone, turning pages in the slow-moving sun that rotates the sky beyond its own cycle. While across the frozen waters of the Pole, Siberia sits looking down on Russia. From here lie Molotov, Severnaya, Semlya, a mysterious chain of connexion toward Russia; Taimyr Lake a matched splash to Hazen where there are no trains, where Vronsky is safe in a dentist's chair, and where Anna is free to read Ellesmere.

At last, again, you think you've found a home.

You search out possible sites for your future grave.

Graveyards overlooking the Pacific from both Canada and Australia are ideal, your dream. At Edberg, the graveyard high above the valley's lip but back far enough to pretend distance. From it the lake is visible, Dried Meat Lake where the summer days waited to be wasted. If you could count on a family plot there, the decision would be simple, taken out of your hands; you could stop wandering, imagining sites for yourself, necessary cordons and fences. Edberg, you thought, was a solution, there in that small, scattered enclosure of prairie grass and tumbleweed, hardly a tree to shelter a tombstone. The road curving past only a scatter of gravel. But you suppose it will never happen, the notion of a family plot, your mother shudders and refuses to be buried there; the coyotes, she says, howl at night, the coyotes lurk around the graves.

> Oh bury me not on the lone prairie
> Where the coyotes howl and the wind blows free
> In a narrow grave...

You find it more civilized than the crowded, rankly elbowing graves of Europe, so close as to catch each other's contagions after death. Some prairie sedge, some buffalo beans. Lying there, satisfied, with your hands crossed over your breast, listening to the coyotes, the same sensation you had as a child lying in the narrow room under the narrow eaves. Yes, a possible gravesite, a place where you can reconcile yourself with your unread childhood.

Or Edmonton, you have thought of Edmonton as a site for buryings, that encircled city where you divided self. Although you have dreamed of flying from the High Level Bridge straight to heaven, although you have woken to the sound of ice in the North Saskatchewan grinding itself open against the banks, there are no gravesites there. No plots, no sacred grounds, no tundra tombstones: lie quietly, breathe a sigh of relief.

Or Calgary, four quadrants offering you succour, a reminder of living, of looming, of the foreland thrust sheets. You have dreamed of buying a plot in the northwest, the fourth fold on Nose Hill, dreamed of sneaking into the Chinese cemetery to vicariously enjoy their ancestors.

You are destined to become ashes. Ashes alone. There are murderers at large.

You have imagined again and again places for your ashes to be scattered to the high winds. The Mackenzie mountains in the Yukon, their sheer red sides inviting the remains of bone. The Coastal mountains outside Stewart, BC, their infinitely green glaciers. The wave-whipped beaches of Pacific Rim, its bleached and splintered tree bones. All possible sites of repose, every one wishes you under/rited there, as ash or flesh, every one offers the pleasure of potential burial, a site where your own grit can join the grit of landscape.

Your wanderings have passed: explorations on site, a site through which to read, to welcome death, early or late.

Anna sleeps and lovers come to murder. The lover persisting your body: persuades/cajoles/entreats. Past sleep, past waking, in the hot commingled juice of arousal, his craving insists. The addict lover lusts, will ford streams and hike mountains of desire in that spiralled hunger when the woman is backed down between his knees, his fatal crouch. A hand on the hand, the knee, the thigh, a judicious hug, an impulse-laden kiss, quick with signification. Routes of seduction: to itself, to lovers, to death.

Anna holds her red bag as talisman, she carries its ubiquity, daring to know her cunt, its lust for reading. Anna trusts her reading and her body: all other persuasions are traducer's inventions, excuses. She reads toward her own capitulation: her lover/her killer/her necrophiliac scribe.

> *That which for nearly a year had been the one absorbing desire of Vronsky's life, supplanting all his former desires; that which for Anna had been an impossible, terrible, but all the more bewitching dream of bliss, had come to pass.*

The woman's skin bleeds naked, her hair unloosed she sinks and falls, the murder is complete. The slow slide of entrance, the body plunging against hers, buttocks contracting, the shallow cleft of knees, her grieving bird-cries preclude the death of ardency. Lovers desire and seduce only to murder and create.

> *Looking at him, she had a physical sense of her degradation and could not utter another word. He felt what a murderer must feel when he looks at the body he has robbed of life…But in spite of the murderer's horror before the body of his victim, that body must be hacked to pieces and hidden, and the murderer must make use of what he has obtained by his crime.*
>
> *And, as with fury and passion the murderer throws himself upon the body and drags it and hacks at it, so he covered her face and shoulders with kisses.*

Anna murdered, you murdered, your body abandoned under its burden of blood and bone, the terrible violation of an iron writing.

You are aroused to saturate a dying fall, an extinguished light, a site in which to sleep. Ellesmere, this high sun-shadowed plateau left holding Lake Hazen in its palm, this islanded woman waiting to be read a justice or a future.

: sleeps dreams under the quick hop of Arctic hares, the yellow glow of Arctic poppies. White nights the sorrowful sheen of a glacial narcolepsy.

Oh Anna.

Writing is an act of appropriation, and I acknowledge the presence and influence of the following books:

Bayley, John, *Tolstoy and the Novel*. Toronto: Clarke, Irwin & Co. Ltd., 1966.

Birney, Earle, "Ellesmereland II," *Ghost in the Wheels*. Toronto: McClelland and Stewart, 1977.

Christian, R. F., editor and translator, *Tolstoy's Letters*. 2 volumes. New York: Scribners, 1978. May 31, 1873, October 19, 1877.

de Courcel, Martine, *Tolstoy: the Ultimate Reconciliation*. Translated by Peter Levi. New York: Charles Scribner's Sons, 1988.

Edmonton Bulletin. Passages appearing in "Edmonton, long division" are quoted from the years 1881-1884.

Evans, Mary, *Reflecting on Anna Karenina*. New York: Routledge, 1989.

MacGregor, J.G., *The Battle River Valley*, Saskatoon: Western Producer Prairie Books, 1976.

Scklovsky, V., *Lev Tolstoy*. Translated by Olga Shartse. Moscow: Progress Publishers, 1978, p. 452.

Tolstoy, L. N., *Anna Karenin*. Translated and with an Introduction by Rosemary Edmonds. Harmondsworth, Middlesex: Penguin, 1977. Passages appearing in "Ellesmere, woman as island" are quoted from this edition, in order: pp. 21, 53, 65, 75, 75, 166, 149, 93, 150, 151, 154, 151, 54, 13, 152, 74, 164, 379, 380, 386-387, 785, 798, 802, 127, 388, 391, 392, 413, 114-115, 802, 674, 382, 784, 802, 812, 165, 165.

Printed on paper
containing over 50%
recycled paper including
5% post-consumer fibre.

Printed in Canada